Thomas' Rescued Heart

The Holliman Brothers
Book 1

By: Jean Marie

ISBN: 13-9798374303094
Imprint: Independently published

Cover design by: Cosmic Letterz
Library of Congress Control Number: 2018675309
Printed in the United States of America

Table of Contents

Chapter 1

Virginia

"I think you've made decent progress, Clarice. How are your nightmares doing?" I asked, eyes only for the dark-skinned woman sitting across from me.

The last thing I'd expected those months ago was to get a new client in the form of her, a woman who'd shot and killed someone in self-defense, but I couldn't say I regretted it. She'd been having nightmares that were steadily increasing in severity and her family had worried.

Until they'd found me.

Most of my patients were here over minor things; the worst I'd had since moving here years ago was the occasional cheating couple trying to work things out, and that was just how I liked it.

I'd had more than enough of the bigger traumas that always seemed to follow major cities.

A flash of him speared behind my eyes, the slimy unwashed blonde hair that always smelled–the only thing that'd kept me from saying anything was professionalism, and even then, it'd been close–and the creepy glint I hadn't understood in his eyes until it was too late.

Ice slid down my spine as I forced the thought away with practiced ease.

He's gone; don't let him ruin your life after you moved to get away.

Refocusing on Clarice, I listened attentively, more than happy for a distraction from my thoughts.

She shifted awkwardly, long black hair swept over her shoulders as she shrugged. "Better, which definitely relieves Vincent. Poor man has been higher strung than me with this whole mess."

That didn't surprise me. The first time she'd come in, her partner Vincent had been with her. He all but oozed worry and protectiveness, admitting later that he'd been the driving force behind Clarice coming to me.

He hated seeing her torn apart, and he'd seen what therapy could do.

It was sweet, seeing those two around one another, and when I smiled at her, it was genuine despite the dark thoughts just out of reach.

"He cares, that's a good thing, and I'm glad you're doing better. How have things been with your family?" I asked, leaning back to relax a bit more. My shoulders ached something fierce since my not at all restful sleep last night and I could only hope today the tension would leak out.

Something in me doubted that, but one could hope.

Immediately, Clarice brightened. "Everyone is abuzz, actually. Vincent's brother Thomas is coming home soon. There's going to be a parade and he's talking about starting a dog rescue with his twin brother Adam and his partner, Helena."

Now that caught my interest.

Sitting forward again, giving up on the attempt to soothe my pulsing shoulders, I questioned. "A dog rescue? That's quite the endeavor."

She nodded, smile stretching the more she talked. "Yeah, I said the same thing. I'm sure you heard about that dog fighting ring?"

I hummed, acknowledging without interrupting. I had, dreadful thing, especially so close to town. I'd hate to think of what those poor animals lived through, and I, for one, whole heartedly supported the idea.

It didn't take a genius to know where those dogs had gone, after all.

Sure enough, Clarice continued.

"Well, Helena is the one who got tangled in it. She's determined to give the dogs a good life, along with whichever other ones she winds up taking care of. Vincent said Thomas was excited to join the last time he talked to him. He's a K9 unit in the Marines."

Immediately, my therapist brain kicked in.

"That'll be good for his adjustment, as long as he doesn't try too much at once." I immediately clapped a hand over my mouth, not meaning for that to come out. "Sorry, I'm in session with you and that was inappropriate," I said, offering an apologetic glance, but she waved it off.

"It's fine; it's not like you're wrong. That's actually something their parents thought of, too, and are relieved by. Apparently, their father had a horrible time readjusting to civilian life. Adam didn't, but Thomas is already having trouble."

I winced internally at that. If he was having trouble while getting out of the service, he was going to be one of the harder cases later. Forcing that thought back, I pulled us back to the topic of the dog rescue.

"Well, I'm sure he'll be fine with such a big family. As for the dog rescue, I might have to stop by and volunteer sometime. I haven't been to something like that in a long time." Which was true. I'd used to make it part of my weekly schedule to volunteer at rescues and shelters in the city. It'd been relaxing, and being around the dogs was a delight.

But then he happened, and everything fell apart.

My stomach soured, but before I could start sliding, Clarice spoke, blessedly dragging me from my thoughts. "I could probably get his number for you to contact? They've been looking for volunteers."

"That sounds nice, and I believe our time is up for today. Feel free to text me his number and I'll talk to him about it later," I said, seeing her out.

She gave a cheery wave and left, a spring to her step I was more than happy to see.

Nothing made me walk taller than watching my patients' burdens drop. No one should have to live with trauma, but if I could help a few people with it, then I'd consider my degree well worth it.

Gathering my things for the day, I went through the motions of locking up behind me and going home. It'd been a long one, not helped at all by my sore shoulders, and I was ready for a hot soak and a cuddle with Bello.

Thankfully, the drive passed quickly, and in no time, I was opening the door to my house, the one-story building comfortable and homey. The second the door shut, the sound of soft pattering on wood floors came, and I barely had time to flick the light on before Bello launched himself at me.

The ball of fur landed squarely in my arms, his head shoving up against my throat as he let out a mighty purr like a miniature lawn mower.

He was my miniature lawn mower, though, and I adored him.

Kicking off my shoes, I stroked down his back, now completely used to the squashed face split with a scar and uneven fur lengths thanks to his previous abusive owner.

I'd forever be grateful for finding him. In my worst times, he'd been my anchor like no other, and I didn't want to think of how lonely the years would have been without him.

"All right, all right. You don't need to be a suck-up; I'm getting your food now." Despite the harsh words, my tone was a low coo, and he responded with another purr that vibrated through my chest.

Setting him down on the stool–he knew not to get onto the counter, but the stool was acceptable–I dug out his canned food and poured it into his bowl. In a blur, he was there, scarfing it down with vigor as I shook my head.

"One would think I never feed you when you do that."

Was it odd that I talked to a cat? Probably, but I never expected an answer back so I'd say I'm mostly safe from insanity.

Mostly.

Sliding a tv dinner into the oven–I didn't have the energy today to cook a real meal–I slumped into the kitchen chair and looked around with a happy sigh.

Clean granite counters shone under the light, the tile floors cold under my feet and clashing well with the dark cherry wood cupboards.

This was my pride and joy of the house: the kitchen. It'd taken me the better part of two years to save up and slowly put this place together, and I regretted not a minute of it.

Everything was just how I imagined it when I'd been a kid thinking about my future.

Well, as my eyes drifted to the empty chair across from mine, I corrected myself. Most of it was how I imagined.

Back then, things had seemed so simple. Work toward my degree–Check. Get a house and turn it into my dream place–Check. Get a cat or dog to keep me company–Check.

Find a relationship? Definitely not check.

Memories of threats, pictures of me changing found on my bed after I'd locked the door and left for work, and so much more trickled through my mind as I let my head sink into my hands.

It'd been years since Steven had played a role in my life, and I still hadn't escaped him.

I hadn't even been in a relationship and had the typical trauma from a bad one! At least then there'd be support groups to go to, people who'd understand. But how many therapists were stalked by former patients to the point of fearing for their lives?

Honestly, the answer was probably higher than I wanted to believe, but the point remained: I was in a smaller group of people, and it made finding support exceptionally difficult.

Maybe I should see a therapist. After all, it's been years, and even now, ice slides up the back of my neck, the feeling of eyes boring into me impossible to ignore. If I was still having these problems now, then therapy would definitely be a good idea.

Though that meant going out of town since I was the only one here...

The oven beeped, announcing my "dinner," and I stood to retrieve it. The hair-raising feeling of being watched didn't fade, and as I plopped down to eat my unappetizing macaroni and cheese, I glanced warily out the window.

Don't do this to yourself, Virginia. He's not here; he's in JAIL. Don't let him take away your happiness.

I repeated it like a mantra, but after I finished and the food sat uneasily in my stomach, I found my way to the window despite logic telling me to get that soak I'd burned for.

Nothing was outside, the lawn just starting to be painted with shadows, but the feeling didn't go away.

Yup, time to see a therapist.

Forcing myself to turn, I made for the bathroom, Bello following behind me as he always did when I was anxious. The cat detested water, as most cats did, but whenever he sensed I was uneasy and I went for a bath, he'd be right there on the toilet seat as if guarding me in my moment of vulnerability.

I adored him for it.

Filling the tub, I stripped and sank into it, sighing in relief when the burn between my shoulders eased. It wouldn't go away until I relaxed, as I knew from experience, and the more time I spent thinking about Steven, the worse it was going to be.

Better to put the man out of mind. He was in a jail cell, where he belonged, and I was states away, where I belonged. Everything was how I'd always wanted it to be and who knows? Maybe I'd even try the dating scene soon.

My stomach rolled uneasily at the thought, memories of all the things Steven had tainted in his psychotic attempts to date me making me drop the thought immediately.

Or not.

As it stood, I probably wouldn't be able to do anything without constantly wanting to look over my shoulder or second guess the person taking me out. That wasn't fair to either of us.

Apparently, dating would have to wait a bit longer yet.

Settling down into the hot water, I sighed. Something told me tonight was going to be a sleepless one. Great, right before I need to meet with someone about volunteering again.

Some things just couldn't be helped.

Reaching out to stroke Bello's ear, I let my worries fade away as I soaked. I'd deal with it all tomorrow. For now, I wanted to enjoy this.

Chapter 2

I stared at the swirling coffee in my mug as if it held all the answers to the universe. Honestly, it felt like it did.

Just like I'd figured, I'd gotten approximately half an hour of sleep last night, and wow, was it biting me today. And of course, just thirty minutes after I'd gotten to sleep, I got a text from Clarice telling me Thomas was back in town and wanted to meet me.

Apparently, he'd come in early, hearing about the parade and hoping to avoid it.

Good luck, buddy. This town was determined, and even if he dodged it now, he probably wouldn't forever.

But that was none of my business. What *was* my business was the meeting I had in about twenty minutes that I still needed to get ready for.

Sending a long glance down my frame, the comfortable pajamas and soft bunny slippers making for a comical picture, I heaved a long sigh and trudged off to my room with my coffee still locked in a death grip.

Sleep or no, I had an appointment to get to, and I wouldn't stand the poor man up, especially since he'd probably need as many volunteers as possible when he and Helena first begin the rescue.

Keeping that thought firmly in mind, I moved through my usual morning routine until the woman staring back at me in the mirror looked more like my usual self.

Neatly combed dark hair was pulled back in a ponytail, a single stubborn strand escaping its hold that I ignored. My white shirt clashed nicely with it, the flowing blouse one of my favorites, and with a final glance down at my slacks to make sure none of Bello's hair got on them, I nodded.

That was as good as I was going to get.

Snagging my keys, I paused long enough to drop another can of food in Bello's bowl before heading out. Clarice said to meet Thomas at the family's martial arts studio, blessedly sending me the address, and now that I thought about it, I didn't think I'd been in there yet.

I'd meant to when I'd first come to town. I wasn't very strong and the idea of anyone scaring me like Steven had put me ill at ease. But work had piled up and the idea had gotten buried. Maybe I would ask about a membership while I was there. If I remembered correctly, Clarice mentioned the studio also had a gym portion.

Thoughts bounced off one another the entire drive over, only stopping when the wheels of my truck stopped outside a white building, the sign showing a man mid-kick with the words "Holliman's Martial Arts."

The building itself was a decent size and kept in good repair, and the second I walked in, the cool brush of air took away the humidity of Texas that never seemed to fade.

Biting back a sigh of relief at that, I looked around.

The inside was tastefully decorated with earthy tones, the distant sound of people training a few rooms over meeting my ears as I looked for a person to talk to. I was supposed to meet Thomas here, but what did Thomas even look like?

After a minute of no one showing themselves, I prepared to text Clarice, asking for a photo or something, only for a woman to come bustling out of a side room, a rag thrown over her shoulder with her eyes mid-roll.

Long black hair slid into gray, kind blue eyes sweeping the room only to freeze when they landed on me. Right behind her, a man came in. As a contrast to her, he had dirty blonde hair turning platinum with striking green eyes, and the smitten smile on his lips didn't fade when he noticed me.

"Ah, we have a new visitor, it appears. I'll leave you be, mi vida." His voice was low, a slight accent twanging through, but before he could make his escape, the woman snagged his hand with another affectionate eye roll.

"Oh no, you don't. You're not getting away with that comment just because she showed up. Once we introduce ourselves, I'll be discussing that. Make no mistake," she said, smile turning impish as he shrugged.

With that, they both made their way over, an almost physical cloud of adoration around them as they stopped a few feet in front of me.

The woman spoke first, a beaming smile that made me feel at home shining up at me. "I'm Penelope Holliman and *this*." She paused to dramatically gesture to the man behind her who dipped his head. "Is my amazing, but sometimes aggravating, husband, Juan."

His cheeks darkened slightly through his olive skin as he cleared his throat. "Such nice introductions you always give. Perhaps I should start doing the same, hmm?"

Before I could find something to say to the admittedly adorable older couple, another voice rang out from behind me, nearly sending me out of my skin.

"It's amazing you guys don't scare off customers like that."

I swung around, only to pause at the chest that was now less than two inches from my nose. Looking up, and up, and up some more, I finally took in the man who spoke.

Despite the words, his tone all but dripped with amusement, a steady affection burning in his eyes as he stared at the couple.

This gave me a chance to take him in uninterrupted. Short, dark hair was cropped nearly to his skull, the curls of his beard making up for the lack of length on his head. He towered over me, thick arms crossed at his chest as he watched with a smile.

But it was only when he turned his eyes to me that everything else faded into the background. Green eyes all but cut through me, the affection fading to something else entirely as he flicked a quick glance down my frame.

Fighting the urge to smooth my shirt, I straightened my spine–not that it did much height-wise–and offered a hand when no one said anything after a moment.

"Hi, I'm Virginia, and I'm here to talk about volunteering at a dog rescue," I said, watching as a flash of understanding flickered across his face. His hand reached out, easily eclipsing mine as he shook gently.

"Ah, you're the woman Clarice raved about." Dimly I noticed the older couple exchange a long glance when he didn't let go of the handshake after a few seconds. To be honest, I wasn't in any hurry for him to.

His grip was warm and firm without being too tight. The innocent touch was welcome, but before my mind could trail to how it could be *not* innocent, I carefully took my hand back and smiled.

"Glad to know I come with high reviews."

Neither of us spoke after that, his eyes boring into me as if looking for something. After a long minute, a throat cleared and we turned in sync to face the knowing twinkle in the elder woman's eyes.

Oooh boy, I knew that look.

We have a matchmaker.

Stepping back to put space between Thomas and me, I listened when she sent me a knowing smile.

"Thomas, I taught you better than that! Use your manners when introducing yourself for the first time to such a beautiful young lady," she said, eyes sharp, and when she flicked another glance between what I now knew to be her son and me, it was all I could do not to groan.

I hadn't come here looking to find a match, no matter how nice the woman attempting it was. Apparently, Thomas caught the vibe as well because he let out a long sigh.

"Ma—" He started, only to be cut off when his father chuckled.

"Give up, *mijo*. You know how she gets when she has something in her head." The words were low and comforting, his wife shooting him a look with a little huff.

"I'm doing nothing…yet. I'm only insisting that my boy use the manners I spent *years* ingraining in him; there is nothing wrong with that. Now then, Thomas?" She put a hand on her hip, an eyebrow raised in challenge, and he turned with his hands raised in surrender.

"All right, all right. No need for that look…" he muttered, facing me with an apologetic glint to his eyes as he spoke. "As my mother has made obvious by now, I'm Thomas. Good to meet you."

I gave him a smile, hoping to show that I didn't mind the meddling. "Right back at you. And good to meet you two as well." I sent the last part to his parents, a flicker of approval showing in Penelope's eyes before she hustled her husband out the door they'd come in.

"Yes, I'll be sure to talk to you more, make no mistake, but for now, I have a husband to talk to. What *was* it you were saying before? Something about my casserole, dear?" Her tone dipped into a sickly sweet threat and Juan smiled, a hint of uncertainty clear as he linked arms with his wife and tried to dig himself out of his hole.

"There is absolutely nothing wrong with your casserole, *mi vida*. I was merely saying—" His voice cut off as he walked away, Penelope watching with a knowing and amused curl to her lips. Once they were out of sight, Thomas heaved a sigh.

"Sorry about them. I only just got back but they're…honestly exactly what I remember them being like." Despite the embarrassment lingering in his tone and the blade of aggravation hidden under it, he still smiled and shook his head.

The overall air of "they're crazy and I love them" made me smile. This was the family I'd always wanted growing up, and seeing it in action was something else entirely. In all my years as a therapist, I'd seen so much hate in families, or even couples, that I'd started to think this didn't exist.

It was a breath of fresh air being around them.

Waving his concern off, I chuckled. "It's not a big thing, honestly. Seeing two people who are so obviously in love with each other is nice. Not to mention even when she was teasing you, it was obvious she adores you. Also nice."

He paused, breaking from the affectionate stare to look at me with curiosity.

Shit, did I overstep? Before I could apologize, his eyes softened, and his entire demeanor shifted. "Ah, Clarice mentioned you were a

19

therapist as well. I'm sure you hear some real horror stories. When I think about it like that, I can see why they'd be refreshing."

Oh good, I didn't offend him. Wiping away the brief panic, I nodded. "I always wanted a family like that so it was kind of surprising to actually see it in action. Not bad though, definitely not bad." I trailed off, a sharp prick of wistfulness twisting inside my chest as I drifted back in time to when I'd dreamed of having that.

Having parents who adored one another openly, adored *me* openly, and maybe even a partner like that further down the line. It burned, knowing I'd never have it.

"What was your family like?" Thomas asked, dragging me from my thoughts just as a dull mist started covering my eyes. Not that this new topic was any better for it…still, I'd gotten used to answering, and without a hint of emotion, I told him the truth.

"Don't know. The orphanage head told me I was dropped on the porch with a blanket and a stuffed animal. Nothing else. By the time she found me in the morning, I was pretty much a block of ice," I said, tone completely neutral, and I watched as Thomas jerked back with wide eyes.

"Jesus, Mary, and Joseph. I'm sorry I asked…" Genuine remorse colored his tone, and I automatically waved it away.

"It's fine. It's not like I told you to butt out. I'm used to people asking and I don't mind it anymore." Back when I was a kid, I had, though. Hearing the taunts from the kids at school over me being an orphan was rough, constant reminders of what I *didn't* have ripping me to shreds some days, but I'd made it through.

Aging out of the system was never a good feeling, but at least it was behind me now. Forcing back the swirling pain in my gut, I turned more toward him and listened when he cleared his throat and asked another question, this one hitting a bit closer to home.

"Did you…ever get adopted by a nice family?"

Hesitance all but oozed from his voice and I bit back a sigh. He was trying to make conversation and was failing miserably, but I couldn't blame him. I didn't exactly act as if the topic was hurting me.

"No, I aged out. Did you want to talk about volunteering?" I changed the subject, already tired of talking about my morbid past.

He caught the obvious change and went along with it without hesitation. "Yeah, yeah. That's a good idea. Helena is the mastermind behind it all but she asked me to keep an eye out for volunteers too. Mostly we'll need help in the mornings, feeding and walking the dogs."

I nodded along, mentally going over my weekly schedule before offering, "I could probably commit to at least two days a week for about four hours, if that works?" Mondays and Thursdays were my late start days at the office, and usually, the workload was light, perfect for volunteering.

"Yeah, any time you can spare is appreciated. A lot of the dogs will be in rough condition so we'll need to get a vet on board at some point, but for now, we just need as many hands on deck as possible," he said, eyes trailing everywhere but me.

Silence passed as he resolutely avoided my eyes, but before I could ask if something was wrong, he cursed under his breath and finally met my gaze again. Regret sat heavy in green eyes as he spoke.

"I'm sorry about before, bringing up the past. My head is still not on straight but that's no excuse."

One of his hands rose to rub the back of his head, guilt clear even as a small smile curled my lips. So he was a sweetheart; good to know.

I patted his arm, ignoring the traveling tingles moving up my hand, and soothed. "It's fine. You're not the first or the last person to ask about it. Besides, I'm over it. As for you still having your head in the wrong place, I'd say you're doing pretty well so far. I've seen plenty of war vets the day after they come home, and trust me, they're in much worse shape than you."

He paused, considering that, before giving a nod. "True. A few of my buddies, in particular, were bad. I've got my issues, but…not like that." The dark tone sent a chill down my spine, and on instinct, I grabbed one of my cards and handed it to him.

"Here, if they ever need someone to talk to, give them by number. I'm used to handling veterans, so they won't be a bother," I said, making sure my tone stayed strong.

His eyes widened in surprise before something warm lit in them, his hand gently taking my card with a nod. "I'll be sure to tell them that. They live in different states, but it still might make a difference. Thank you."

I shrugged, ignoring the warmth blooming in my chest as I did. "It's my job and I wouldn't want them to...slide." I chose the last word carefully, but Thomas's face darkened in understanding.

Veterans had some of the worst mental health problems I'd seen in the business when they came back from the war, and the numbers for how many couldn't take it were heart-wrenching. If the terror I could just see in the back of his eyes was any indication, Thomas knew those numbers well and feared for his friends.

I could understand that.

The last thing I expected was for him to shuffle in place and ask, "Can I have two more cards? I have three friends that worry me and I'd prefer to just send them your card so they have the information in hand...should they need it."

Immediately, I pulled out two more and handed them over.

I'd never tried therapy over the internet, but if it came down to it, I'd do my best. Thomas's shoulders eased, his hand disappearing to tuck the cards into his pocket before focusing on me again.

"Thank you. It means a lot."

I hummed, not sure how to respond. Again silence passed between us, but this time something else lingered under the surface. I couldn't put my finger on what it was, and after a long minute of staring at each other, Thomas cleared his throat.

"Right, volunteering. I'll call Helena later and let her know you're on board. I'm sure she'll be giving you a call as well at some point. She likes talking to people and getting to know them personally."

Sounded like the kind of woman I'd get along with just fine.

"I'll be waiting for her call then. Any idea when the rescue should be open and ready for business?" I asked, watching as Thomas shrugged apologetically.

"Not at the moment. Helena and I are still working out all the kinks, but once we do, I'll give you a call." He trailed off, the topic petering out as a heavy silence permeated the air. Awkwardness slid up my spine, prodding me to say something *anything*.

This was why I never did well in social situations. Once the main topic at hand was dealt with, I couldn't think of another one…

When Thomas started shifting between his feet, just as uncertain as me, I forced down the discomfort and tried for a safe subject change. It wasn't often I got to talk to people outside work, and he seemed nice. I could at least try to make a friend.

With that in mind, I asked, "Clarice mentioned you were just getting back. How does it feel to be home?"

For once, I wasn't asking as a therapist but as a regular person, and Thomas raised a hand to rub at the back of his neck.

"Decent, overwhelming at times, but still good. A lot has changed since the last time I was here; most of my old friends have moved to bigger cities, but I'd say I'm adapting well," he answered, eyes not meeting mine.

Apparently, I'm not the only one who has trouble keeping friends. Well, maybe this would be good for both of us then.

Without thought, I offered, "I've only been here a few years, but I have a decent idea of the layout now. If you want we could go for a day on the town and see what all has changed? I think there's a few new businesses here and the town fifteen minutes away has *definitely* added more venues."

Thomas blinked, taken by surprise at the offer, but before I could take it back–the crawling embarrassment moving up my back demanding it–he nodded.

"That would be nice. How about lunch then? You can bring me up to speed while we eat, and afterward, we can look around. The town isn't exactly big so it shouldn't take that long and I'm of the firm belief that food makes everything better."

A light teasing dipped through his tone and my lips quirked up in response. "That sounds fine to me. Do you want to head out now?"

He nodded, his arm moving out in silent offering. That was... not something I was used to, but I took it without a word. The warm muscles bunched under my palm, distracting me as he led us toward the doors.

I caught a glimpse of Penelope's head peeking out from a side room, her lips curled into a knowing and excited grin that made me groan internally. Matchmaker, right.

Putting that to the side to worry about later, I focused on Thomas as the conversation fell into the sports teams of the town over from ours. I didn't have a lot of information on this, but what little I did, he seemed happy with.

It'd been what felt like forever since the last time I'd gone out to lunch with someone, and something about Thomas made jitters of nerves dance up my spine, settling in my stomach like a wriggling worm. Which made no sense since we were going out as *friends*.

How long had it been since I'd wanted companionship outside of my work?

At least three years, I knew that much. Shoving aside the dark thoughts threatening to bash down my current happiness, I settled my resolve.

I was allowed to have friends, and Thomas seemed nice. We'd go out to lunch and have a lovely time. Then I'd go home to my Bello and go back to work tomorrow. This wasn't some life-changing thing, just lunch with a friend, and I'd treat it as such.

No matter how much my nerves wanted to make it into something it wasn't.

Chapter 3

The building we pulled up to was small, but its size did nothing to detract from the gorgeous picture it made.

Red brick walls were hidden behind the wide array of flowers of seemingly every color. Arches lined the walkway up to the door of the building, crawling vines covering them and forming an almost magical entryway.

In short, it was stunning.

"Every single woman who has seen this place has reacted in the exact same way; it's starting to be funny," Thomas said, breaking me from my thoughts as a light dusting of pink colored my cheeks.

He'd slid out of the driver's seat while I'd been stuck in my dumbfounded stupor, and now he stood outside my door, mouth curled in an easy smile as he opened it for me.

Yet another thing I'd have to get used to with him. Apparently, the manners didn't stop with the arm thing.

Gingerly sliding out, I took his arm again as I huffed, responding to the previous quip. "I don't blame them. It's gorgeous. I've never seen any kind of restaurant like this before."

The front of it was just so *alive*.

Thomas nodded, guiding us in where the same warm, earthy tones as the martial arts studio greeted us. Booths lined the walls, a few couples scattered here or there eating various dishes that all looked amazing.

Hopefully, it tasted as good.

"Yeah, Finn worked hard on this place and asked for Ma's help a lot. Gotta admit, it turned out great," Thomas said, once again yanking me from my thoughts. Before I had a chance to ask who Finn was, or how he knew Thomas's mother, a man came bounding out of the kitchen entrance, his cheeks split in a wide smile.

Kind eyes all but glowed with energy as the brunette came to a stop in front of us; his frame was slimmer than Thomas by a good bit, but even from here, I could see the definition underneath the apron he wore.

His arms were lined with muscle, too, hinting at a power one wouldn't expect from his size as he threw his arms around Thomas and *picked him up* in a hug. Instinctively stepping back to give them room, I watched in shock as the considerably smaller man hefted Thomas as if he weighed nothing.

He dropped him in the next second, stepping back and giving me a clear view of his face. Dark stubble covered his chin, a mustache completing the look as short brown hair tussled with his sudden move.

All in all, he was attractive. Despite that dispassionate observation, not an ounce of interest flared, to my surprise. Everything about the man seemed my usual type, from his facial hair right down to his leaner frame, but I felt...nothing.

Well, not nothing.

His obvious exuberance made a spark of amusement cleave through my chest, but the attraction I'd expected wasn't there.

That *was* weird, but I'd analyze it later.

Finally, the other man seemed to realize Thomas wasn't here alone because his smile faded a bit as pure disbelief took its place. Before I had a chance to blink, the shorter male spun on Thomas and smacked his shoulder.

"Not even back in town a week and you've already got a beautiful woman on your arm. Jesus, how do you *do* it?" His voice was low, a teasing undertone to it as Thomas shook him off with a grunt.

The compliment also didn't go over my head as warmth crawled up my cheeks. It wasn't often I was called beautiful, but I'd take it where I got it.

Before I could thank him for that, Thomas spoke up with a roll of his eyes, shoving the smaller man playfully. "It's called making friends with people, Finn. I know you've heard of it. And we ain't here for that, knucklehead. I asked her to bring me up to speed on everything that's changed since I left and there's no better place than over lunch."

The now dubbed Finn stepped back with a shrug, his smile coming back as he easily ducked under Thomas's elbow. "And you couldn't have asked one of *us* to do that? You know, your brothers that

29

have lived here the entire time you were gone and thus were there for all the changes?"

The teasing tone didn't drop even as a light flush worked across Thomas's cheeks, almost getting lost in his beard. It was a nice look on him, but before I could say so, Thomas huffed.

"Finn, drop it. You haven't introduced yourself yet and she's probably already getting a bad first impression of you."

Actually, I wasn't. I had more than a bit of experience with jokers like he seemed to be, and honestly? It was a breath of fresh air. I couldn't say that, though, before Finn turned to me with a massive grin and bowed at the waist, an arm extending theatrically as he pulled up into a wink.

"Can't have that, can we? I'm Finn Holliman, brother to this mountain of a man, and five others. You'll probably meet them if you wind up hanging out more with us. And you are?"

Choking back my surprise at the thought of having *seven* sons—Penelope must have had the patience of a saint–I offered my hand and responded.

"Virginia Bren. Good to meet you."

Just like with Thomas, Finn's handshake was steady but not bruising. Once he let me go, he stepped back with a nod. "Good to meet you too. Rare to see Thomas over there making friends but I'm glad he's finally branching out."

Turning to face his brother again, Finn teased, "How's that mutt of yours doing?"

Thomas shook his head, used to his brother's antics, as he answered. "Naomi is fine, happy to be relaxing at home instead of running through a war zone, I can tell you that."

Distantly I remembered Clarice mentioning Thomas's spot in the Marine K9 units. Maybe I'd ask some day to meet Naomi, but today was definitely not it.

"She's going to be so spoiled, I hope you know. Even without whatever treats you give her, Vincent's woman Clarice has two kids that *adore* animals. I can already see the table scraps headed her way now." Finn said, bringing me back to the present as Thomas rolled his eyes but didn't dispute that. Instead, he offered his arm to me again and nodded back to the booths.

"Yeah, yeah, whatever. Now let's get seated, I didn't bring her here *just* to meet you and I haven't eaten lunch yet," he said, gently tugging me back towards the booths as Finn followed, waving off one of the servers who made it as if to get our table.

Instead of sitting, like I expected, Finn leaned a hip against the table and pulled out a notebook. "All right, what'll it be? I don't have the garlic and cheese sauce anymore, just a heads up. But I have a killer alfredo you'd probably dig."

Thomas nodded, not bothering to pick up the menu. "Yeah, but wait to start on mine until Virginia figures out hers. Until then, I'll have a coke."

Both heads turned to me in the next second and I looked through the drinks portions of the menu. "I'll go for a water."

Finn nodded, noting it down before sauntering off with a wink over his shoulder to Thomas and a cheery, "I'll be back soon. No need to stop your *date*." His voice went sing-song on the last word and Thomas flipped him off.

A flash of a kid nearby had me quickly covering the middle finger, to Thomas's confusion.

Heat inched up my cheeks before I nodded to the kid passing by, curious eyes watching us as only a kid could while their parents sent a glare Thomas's way.

The man cringed, quickly putting down his hand as he looked away. Instead of pulling back from me, like I expected, he flipped his hand over and gave mine a squeeze of thanks.

"That was close. I'm so used to my buddies in the Marines that I gotta remind myself I'm not there anymore," he muttered, the warmth of his hand around mine lingering as tingles worked up my arm. When they seemed to spread further, I gently disentangled us and nodded.

"Yeah, I didn't think you'd want to be responsible for teaching anyone's kid that particular hand sign," I teased, delighted when his flush increased.

Oh, I was going to love seeing that the more we hung out.

Before I could comment on it, though, he cleared his throat and gestured to the menu. "I don't know what you like but Finn usually has a decent selection."

Seeing the request for a subject change, I went with it. Hopefully, I'd have plenty of opportunities in the future to tease him. No need to pile it all on at once.

Flipping through the menu, I scanned the options before nodding. "I think I'll go with the hamburger."

Hamburgers were usually a safe bet, no matter where they were cooked.

Thomas hummed, setting the menus to the side before focusing back on me. "So, you mentioned moving here. How did you even *find* this place on a map? And why'd you want to move if you don't mind my asking?" he asked.

I licked my lips, memories of what, or more accurately *who* chased me away threatening to rise as I pushed them down. No reason to send the man running with my horror stories; besides, I'd given the half-truth version of this answer so many times now that it flowed off my tongue without hesitation.

"Finding this place was a happy accident that involved a dart and a map. As for why I moved, I wanted a change. I'm from New York City and it never seemed to quiet down." I shrugged. "Say what you will about this place; it's definitely *quiet*."

And with my job as a therapist, that was a God send. No more beaten and abused spouses coming in, begging me to answer why their loved one had changed so dramatically as if I could ever know such a thing.

No more couples therapies that almost always delved into screaming matches, the pair's toxicity clear to anyone with eyes as they verbally ripped into one another.

No more being exposed to the hate that overflowed liberally from the big city while people looked to me to fix it for them.

Here, the worst I had was Clarice, and the woman was an angel in comparison to other patients I'd seen.

I had needed to get away from New York and everything in it, and where better than here? The good ole South.

Looking up, I froze at the intent stare Thomas leveled on me. His eyes bore in as if able to see the rest of my answer, but before I could get too uncomfortable with the stare, he dropped it and looked away.

"Fair enough. I couldn't imagine being in the big city even *before* my time in the Marines. Now?" He shuddered. "I'd never make it. The noise and people would drive me insane."

That was a common feeling from veterans, at least it seemed to be from the ones I'd talked to. Putting that to the side, I nodded. "Understandable. What made you choose to go into the Marines?"

Thomas leaned back a bit to that, mouth softening at the edges as he gave a small smile. "My father. He was in the military for most of my childhood. He was honorably discharged when Dick—sorry, Richard—was a kid. When I got out of school, I didn't really have any kind of calling and then a recruiter showed up one day and it just seemed right."

The slip with Richard's name pulled a snort from me. "Richard. I take it that's another brother of yours. Dear God, to have seven boys... Your mother is a saint, and you won't convince me otherwise," I said, smiling when Thomas's eyes lit up, and a wide grin crossed his lips.

"Oh, trust me, I'm right there with you. The testosterone must have been something else, but somehow she kept us all in line. And when Richard was growing up, we definitely didn't make that easy on her."

My brow rose to that. Seemed like there was a story. Thomas noticed my brow and grimaced, some of the warmth draining as he sighed.

"Yeah, we weren't exactly the best brothers to Richard for a while there. To put it plainly, we were jealous. Dad had been gone for most of our lives, and then along came Richard, who got to grow up with Dad being *there* for everything. All the school ceremonies and awards things, all the sports days, and pretty much everything my brothers and I had wanted him to be there for *us* growing up." He shrugged, not making any excuses.

"We were assholes for a while, not gonna lie. Mom eventually dragged us into a discussion and we aired it all. Made Dad feel like shit, but after that, things got better." Thomas cringed, "Still doesn't excuse the way we treated Richard, though. He forgave us a long time ago, but still..."

I nodded. Just because he forgave them didn't mean they forgave themselves. Honestly, I was just impressed they'd managed to stitch it all back together so well. Things like that were known for splitting apart families at the seams.

Without thought, I reached over and gave his hand a squeeze. "At least you're aware that what you did was wrong. You didn't just sweep it under the rug and call it done. You'd be surprised how many people do that and later have it bite them."

He paused, eyeing my hand for the briefest minute, before curling his back around mine. The weight was comforting, calluses on his palm rubbing against me as he hummed.

"Yeah, Ma made sure we all took full responsibility for our shit— sorry, language." He winced at that before I waved off the apology with ease.

"Trust me, I've heard worse," I said, watching as the grimace didn't fade.

"Not the point. Even if you're okay with it, I was taught better. Besides, Ma would be after me with a wooden spoon if she heard me talking like that in a family place like this." He nodded to where a family sat not two booths away, kids happily distracted while their parents watched on with amused expressions.

I could understand that, and yet again, I found myself impressed by Penelope Holliman. I'd never seen manners like this before, and to think she did it mostly on her own?

Amazing.

Finn sauntered back to the table not two minutes later, smile still firmly in place as he prodded. "You two ready to order?"

I gave him mine, watching as he wrote it down deftly before moving back to the kitchen. Once he was out of earshot, I turned back to Thomas and smiled. "If you want, after this, we can take a walk down Main Street? Most of the shops are there so you'll be able to see what's changed."

He nodded, leaning back as the conversation settled into an easy flow. If everything went as smoothly as this, then I could see us becoming fast friends.

Chapter 4

The food was every bit as amazing as the decorations, and by the time we left, I was pleasantly full and fighting off a nap. Something Thomas noticed but didn't comment on as he offered an arm again.

Smart man.

Now we walked down Main Street arm in arm, his towering frame occasionally pointing out a shop he didn't remember or one he did. It was nice.

If only I could get the squishy feeling in my stomach to settle down, then it'd be perfect.

Having Thomas so close, his arm wound comfortably with mine, was wreaking havoc on me in a way no one else had in…ever. I wasn't the woman who got things like this, that wiggly warmth in her stomach when a man led her down the street.

It was safer that way.

Even now, memories of Steven and all the twisted things he did plagued me, making my skin itch anytime that odd little warmth started in my gut. This was dangerous. For whatever reason, Thomas was different than anyone else I'd been around.

He made me feel things I shouldn't, especially not for someone I only just met, and the smart thing to do would be to cut this off now before the...infatuation had a chance to grow.

Right now, it was just uncomfortable, easily ignored with some practice, but I doubted it would stay that way for long. The last thing I needed was to fall for a man who probably wasn't interested in anything other than getting settled back home.

Now, if I could just get that feeling to settle, I'd be on the right path.

The heat beat down on us, the air thick as if walking through soup, and in no time, it started to get to me. Every step felt like it was weighed down in cement, and every so often, the world dipped sideways: not a good sign.

I hadn't been drinking enough water lately, apparently. Before I could ask to cut the day short, or bring it inside, my heel caught on an uneven stone in the pavement and sent me toppling forward with a yelp.

Bracing for the collision with the hard asphalt, I waited.

Only for it not to come.

An arm snagged around my waist, abruptly stopping my momentum as Thomas tugged me back up to stand next to him. Worry painted his features as he looked me over, brow dipping further at whatever he saw.

"Are you all right?" he asked, tone low and soothing.

Forcing my legs to hold my weight, I nodded. "Yeah, just not enough water. I'm usually pretty good about that, but things have been…insane lately."

With my sleepless nights and work, I hadn't been drinking as much as I should, as proven now. Giving my best attempt at a smile, I shrugged. "I'll be fine; just give me a minute."

Instead of agreeing, he did the last thing I expected; he led me to a bench and gently prodded me down to it.

"Here, I'll get some water from the café a bit back. Dehydration is nothing to mess with," he said, already turning and moving before I had a chance to tell him it wasn't necessary.

Watching his back as he all but ran away, I leaned into the bench and sighed. It wasn't that big of a thing, but I could appreciate how serious he took it.

Stretching my legs, ignoring the slight shake and twinge they gave, I sighed. *Note to self, add more water bottles around the house.*

I usually forget when I don't see the bottle for a while, which leads to having them *everywhere* in my house, but if it was that or dehydration…

Eyeing the direction Thomas left, I almost considered following him. A café sounded like a nice place to rest, but before I could haul myself back onto my feet, a shadow covered me.

Slowly looking up, ignoring the relief of not being in direct sunlight anymore, I met the worried gaze of a stranger.

The man stood far enough away that he wasn't crowding me but close enough that his shadow stayed directly over me. Jeans slung low on his hips, paired with a button-up that clung to his frame like a second skin. Short brown hair was cropped nearly to his skull, a dusting of stubble covering his jaw, and worried eyes locked on me.

"Are you all right? I saw my brother take off like a bat out of hell," he said, voice a low rumble.

Ah, another one of his brothers. I guess that meant I'd met three of them now. Giving my best attempt at a smile through the irritating heat sapping away at my energy, I nodded.

"I'm fine, just a bit dehydrated, and he was running to get water. He didn't give me a chance to tell him it wasn't necessary," I said, watching as the man snorted.

"Yup, that's Thomas. Always was the one to prefer action to words. He should be back soon. In the meantime, introductions. Hi, I'm Richard. For the love of all that's holy in the universe, please don't call me Dick. I get it enough from my brothers."

Ah, so *this* was the youngest Thomas had talked about earlier. Considering how he'd spoken as if Richard had been tortured by him and the rest of the siblings, I'd expected the man to be more surly. Maybe a bit broody.

While he wasn't a walking ray of sunshine, he also wasn't a storm cloud. And to top it off, he shook his head and smiled at the direction Thomas had left. Whatever grudge he may have had in the past was long behind him. Anyone who saw him could see that.

Offering a hand, I nodded, remembering his request. "Sure. I'm Virginia. Nice to meet you. I've heard a bit about you."

At that, Richard's brows went up, his hand snaking out to shake mine as he snorted. "All about how I was the pest younger sibling always underfoot, no doubt."

It was hard to think of anyone with his height as being "underfoot," but I shook it off. "No, actually. He did mention that you were the youngest, though."

Richard hummed, eyeing me as if he knew there was more than that, but he didn't push. "Surprising, then again, it isn't as if you'd asked Finn. *He* would have taken great joy out of telling you every embarrassing thing I've done since I was five."

His grimace was cute, his nose scrunching up at the thought, but before I could ask more about the rest of his siblings, the sound of footsteps came again, and Thomas jogged back to our side.

He paused, surprised to see his brother, before offering me a water bottle. "Here, sorry it took so long."

I sipped on the water, ignoring the familiar plastic taste, and watched as the brothers faced one another, Richard still using himself as a sunblock for me.

"Didn't expect to see you in town today. Thought you were working?" Thomas asked, arm coming out to clasp his brother's shoulder. Richard shrugged, dragging his brother into a hug before releasing him just as quickly.

"I work later. Heard through the grapevine that you were walking around with a woman after going to Finn's place, so I wanted to meet her before work," Richard said, ignoring the groan Thomas gave.

"By grapevine, you mean Ma."

Richard nodded, a smile twitching up his lips. "Yup, she's all sorts of happy right now. Vincent went and got a woman. Now she's all set to get the rest of us hitched. Yay." His tone dripped into something sharper on the last word, the previous teasing long gone.

Apparently, I wasn't the only one to notice.

Thomas sighed. "She probably won't get after you too much if it's any consolation. Not after Scarlet."

Richard stiffened to stone, mouth twisting into a hard line as he took a step back, the sun's rays hitting me again as he looked away.

"No, she's been eyeing me in particular. You know she hates my…sleeping habits," he said, stealing a glance at me from the corner of his eyes. It took me a minute to decipher what it meant, but when I did, I fought the urge to roll my eyes.

I'd thought the name Richard sounded familiar, and now I knew why. Richard Holliman, resident deputy, was a well-known *ladies man*. If the rumors–and his words–were to be believed, it was a rare night that he spent alone.

On the bright side, all the women who'd said such things all had glowing reports of him, reports that I'd really not wanted to hear, but that was life.

Before I could stop it, I snorted. "Yeah, mothers generally don't like hearing that kind of thing. Good luck on dodging it, though, she was even giving *me* matchmaker eyes before we left and I'm not her kid."

Not anyone's kid, that acidic little voice at the back of my head hissed before I shoved it down. Thomas winced, probably remembering those eyes from earlier, as Richard made a noise of sympathy.

"Sounds like she's got her eye on adopting you through one of us. I'm not the only one who'll need luck in dodging that. If you actually have a serious aversion to the whole matchmaking thing, I advise saying so plainly, bluntly, politely, and up front. As quickly as you can. Ma loves doing stuff like this, but she's also *never* crossed that line," Richard said, soothing some of the nerves boiling low in my veins.

At least there was that.

Grappling for a change in subject, I gripped the only one that came to mind. "So who is Scarlet and why should she disqualify you?"

Immediately, the air went icy cold, Richard's eyes shutting down in record time. Thomas cleared his throat, about to step in, but Richard raised a hand and cut him off with a hard smile.

"It's fine. She'll probably hear it around town soon anyway. I prefer people ask and hear it from me so it can't get twisted."

Awareness crawled up my neck, the distinct feeling that I'd just stepped into something very private making my skin itch.

"You don't have to say anything if it's personal," I offered, but Richard shook his head.

"It's fine. I hear it from everyone in town so it's not like I'm not used to it. Scarlet was a woman I dated years ago. Things seemed to be good, but when I was starting to make plans to propose, she broke things off. Wouldn't let me get a word in edgewise to ask just what was going on, even did it over a *note*."

He scoffed, old pain clear even as he tried to hide it. "I haven't been too interested in trying relationships again since that, and Ma knows it. Or at least she did. Apparently, she's had enough of my habits, and with our eldest brother settled down, she's going to look at the rest of us now."

Ouch, no wonder he'd avoided relationships. While my history with them wasn't great by any means—hello stalker—at least I'd never had to deal with *that*.

Without a thought, I patted his arm. "Sorry to hear that. If it's any consolation, she missed out. From what little I've seen of you, Finn, Adam, and Thomas, you're all great guys. Anyone would be lucky to have you."

I didn't realize how that came out before Thomas shifted awkwardly next to us, muttering just loud enough for us to hear. "Should I give you two a room?"

Heat burst across my cheeks, Richard's too, I noticed, as I weakly smacked Thomas's side.

"Oh, don't start. I'm not on the lookout for a relationship either and I'd appreciate you *not* giving your lovely mother any ideas. I was just saying that you all are *nice*, take the compliment," I huffed, watching as Thomas's shoulders eased, though why they'd tensed up in the first place was beyond me.

Richard snorted, pulling me away from my thoughts as he sent his brother an amused look. "She kinda reminds me of Mom, bossy but you can't help but listen to her."

I wasn't sure whether or not to take that as a compliment.

Richard snuck a glance at his watch before making a noise of surprise. "Apparently, it's later than I thought it was. Time to get home and get ready for work. Hope to see you again soon, Virginia."

He paused at Thomas, "And it's good to have you back too." Another quick hug passed before the man turned and walked off, leaving Thomas and me alone again.

Something was different now, the air was heavier, and for the life of me, I couldn't understand why. I also didn't have a chance to investigate before Thomas offered his arm. "You feeling up to walking more or do you think we should call it a day and come back to this later?"

I wanted to continue, but if the shaking in my legs and faint dizziness still clouding my head was any indication, my body was giving me a big "no." Biting back a sigh, I reluctantly answered.

"Maybe another day. I'm feeling a bit wobbly now and the last thing you need is me passing out on you." It hadn't happened in a long time, and I hoped to keep that track record going.

Thomas nodded, leading us back to the car as he spoke. "There's always another day. Besides, from what we've seen everything is mostly the same. Maybe next time I can show *you* around. I still remember a few of the old hiking trails that had stunning views. If you'd be interested?"

I perked up at the thought. It'd been years since I'd gone on a hike and the idea of going with Thomas made it all the more appealing, though I wouldn't be analyzing why that was.

"Sure, I should be off again in a few days. I could text you then?" I offered, climbing into the car with one of Thomas's hands cradling the base of my spine. I hadn't realized how big his hand was until now. It almost spread across my entire lower back when he splayed his fingers out.

Every inch of skin he touched tingled with awareness, the buzzing warmth sliding south before I quickly shook it off and buckled in. *Not the time for this*, I reminded myself.

His voice dragged me back to the present as he moved for the driver's side. "That's fine. I'll give you my number once we get back. You feeling any better?"

The last question caught me by surprise and I nodded dumbly. I was, somewhat, though it'd take the rest of the day and a lot more water before I'd dare go out in the heat again.

Thomas hummed, pleased with that, as he started that car. "Good."

And with that, silence hit. Not the suffocating kind I was used to, thankfully. This was comfortable, having the opportunity to just *be* with someone without having to keep a conversation rolling. If the small smile tugging Thomas's lips was any sign, he thought so too.

Unfortunately, we pulled up to the studio in no time at all. Our comfy silence shattered as yet again Thomas—somehow—managed to beat me to my door and open it. The man had super speed or something...

He sent me a knowing smile but said nothing as he offered a hand, helping me out of the truck and back to my own not three yards away. Once I was settled in the driver's seat, he offered his phone. "Do you want to enter it or should I?"

Without a word, I took it, putting my number in deftly before handing it back. I almost—*almost*—made a joke about this being the first time in a long time that I'd gotten an attractive man's number, but logic thankfully came in to save the day.

No flirting with him, he probably isn't interested.

Keeping that thought at the forefront of my mind, I watched as he looked around, looking for something to say, before sighing.

"I'm not great with stuff like this, but...I had fun today. Thanks for the walk. Hopefully, next time, you'll be feeling better."

Yeah, the almost passing out was definitely something I could happily *not* do.

I went to respond, but before I could, Penelope breezed out the doors of the studio, that glint still firmly in her eyes as she swept a knowing smile my way. Heat slapped across my cheeks as Thomas let out a little sigh, knowing what kind of teasing lay ahead.

Sure enough, his mother stopped a few feet away and asked, "So did you two have fun? Finn couldn't stop talking about you two and how *adorable* you looked."

The heat in my cheeks spread to Thomas's as he faced his mother with a groan. "Mom, you know how he is. Don't start."

His mother hummed but turned to me. "All teasing aside, it was nice to meet you. I hope to see you more often around here." And with that, she went back inside, though the look she shot Thomas practically screamed of another conversation for him on the horizon.

Once we were alone, I gave him an apologetic glance. "I feel like I should apologize, but I don't know what for."

He let out a gusty sigh. "Nothing to apologize over, just Mom being Mom. Anyway, you should get out of here before she decides to start again."

I kind of felt like I was abandoning him, but if he minded, I doubt he would have told me to go. Forcing back the slight guilt, I nodded, starting the car before giving my goodbye.

"I'll do that. Once I get home, I'll check my schedule too. We'll have to plan that hiking day."

The light pink dusting across his cheeks faded, a genuine smile slowly unfurling as he stepped back and watched my truck pull away.

"Can't wait."

I barely caught his response over the sound of gravel and tires, but a flash of warmth twisted in my stomach.

He wasn't the only one who couldn't wait.

Chapter 5

The house seemed even emptier than normal when I got back. Which was ridiculous; one day out with Thomas shouldn't make that big of a difference. I wasn't alone; I had Bello.

And speaking of him, where was he?

The familiar patter of paws and claws on wood didn't come, and he didn't wheel the corner in a blur for his usual cuddles either. Setting down my keys, I called out. "Bello? Here, kitty, kitty."

Again, no answer.

Slowly making my way through each room, my dread steadily grew when I couldn't find him. Once I stood back in the entryway, my heart squeezed as the adrenaline started pumping through my veins.

It's fine. He probably hid somewhere, I tried to reason with myself.

But after another, more thorough look without finding him, panic started clawing at my chest.

Where could he be? I'd closed all the windows before I left and —

A flash of movement caught my attention, my head snapping up to see the kitchen window, which I *distinctly remembered closing,* opened just enough for Bello to slip through. My heart dropped to my shoes as

I raced over, looking through the small square in the hopes that Bello hadn't gone far.

No luck.

He wasn't on the front lawn or anywhere in sight.

Icy fear climbed up my spine, threatening to wrap its fists around my lungs, but I shoved it down. There was still time before dark. I could find him. He was probably nearby and lounging like he usually did.

Spinning on my heel, I raced for the door again, eyes sharp as I watched every nook and cranny I passed on the street.

Bello was an inside cat; he wasn't used to being outdoors, and I could only imagine the trouble he'd get into.

Again my chest tightened, but before I could sink into heinous "what ifs," my phone blared from my hip. Nearly jumping out of my skin, shaking hands fumbled the phone as I answered the unknown number.

"Hi, this is Virginia but this isn't a great time. If I could call you back?"

A beat of silence came before Thomas's voice hit my ears, concern all but oozing off.

"What happened? You seemed fine when you left."

Shit.

I opened my mouth, trying to figure out just what all to tell him as I looked up and down the small cul de sac for a sign of my furry brat, only to deflate when none was there.

I could use help looking—the sun was already starting to drain me again—and something told me Thomas wouldn't mind...

Biting my lip until I tasted iron, I took a slow breath and explained. "It's going to sound stupid, but my cat is missing. I closed the windows, I *know* I did, but somehow he got the kitchen one open and he's not in the house and—"

The more I talked, the more my lungs tightened and tears burned my eyes. I couldn't lose him; I just couldn't. He'd kept me sane through the entire mess with Steven and it'd crush me to have to come home to that empty house every day.

Thankfully, Thomas cut me off before I could start to really panic.

"All right, take a deep breath. I'm on my way. You sound winded, so you should sit somewhere in the shade. What's your address?"

Ignoring the part of me that insisted I shouldn't involve him in something like this, I rattled it off, listening with a tidal wave of relief as the sound of a truck starting echoed from the other end of the line.

"I'm on my way over, just stay calm until then. We can cover more ground between the two of us. If you have any favorite toys, blankets, or treats of his, get them from the house. I have experience catching runaway cats."

Praise the Lord and all his saints. Apparently, Thomas was a cat wrangler, and right now, I was too relieved to care how funny that title sounded.

"Thank you." My voice was shaky, but the gratitude showed through. Thomas hummed, uncomfortable with that thanks, before giving his goodbyes.

With one last long look around, I moved back to the house to gather the items he'd asked for. Hope flicked to life like a fragile flame, valiantly battling back the fear still choking me.

Bello would be okay. We just had to find him…

Or so I hoped.

Thankfully, it didn't take long for Thomas's truck to pull up outside, the door's slam echoing in the otherwise quiet area.

I had all the things ready he'd talked about, sitting neatly in a box by the door, and I opened the door before he could knock.

His fist was raised to do so, mouth set in a line as worry creased his brow. When he saw me, he dropped his hand and stepped back. "You have everything?"

In answer, I tugged out the box, showing him what was inside it. He nodded, gently taking it and offering his other arm. "Good, let's hurry. He might still be nearby. The weather said we might have a surprise storm, and we'll want to find him before that."

Oh, I hadn't even thought about that. Bello *hated* storms and if he was caught out in one, he'd probably be terrified.

Again, hot tears burned the back of my eyes before I blinked them back. "Sorry, I'm a mess right now. He's—" I almost said "he's my best friend," before I caught myself. That probably wouldn't sound great to anyone else, but Thomas just nodded as if he'd known what I was going to say.

"It's fine, nothing to apologize over. Animals are just as much family as humans are, sometimes even more so. No judgment from me. Heck, Naomi is my everything. I'd be just as frantic if something happened to her."

The understanding tone soothed some of my nerves as he handed me the treats. "Here, call for him and shake the bag. A lot of cats will respond to that, and if that doesn't work, then we'll set up small boxes for him with his toys and blankets. Sometimes that'll get them to stay in one place long enough for you to find him."

I hoped it wouldn't come to that. The sky was already getting clouds, and it wouldn't be long before rain came.

Still, I did as told, listening intently for any signs.

This continued for who knows how long before a loud *CRACK* sounded through the air. I jumped, the roll of thunder taking me by surprise, as Thomas sent a grimace up to the sky.

"We're out of time. We'll have to set up the boxes and hope for the best. Once the storm passes, we can look again, but it's not safe to be out here until then," he said.

I knew that, but even the thought of leaving Bello out here alone struck me to the core.

But there wasn't another option.

Swiping at the tears building again, I nodded, not fighting as Thomas turned us back around. I wanted to, but he was already being nice with helping like this, especially since he didn't know me. I wasn't about to make the poor man sit in the rain too.

Before we could make it more than a few steps, his hand brushed my shoulder, gently stopping me. Through blurry vision, I could just make out his sympathetic frown, everything else too blurred to see as he slid an arm around my shoulders and tugged me against his side.

Warmth bit through the cold pain coating my chest, his frame offering comfort and shelter from the wind that was starting to pick up. Under any other circumstances, I'd pull away. I'd only just met him, and generally, I didn't like people being in my space, but...

Thomas was different.

Having him curled around me like this made me feel *safe*, and right now, I could use more of that.

So I let my head fall to his shoulder, exhaustion chewing on my bones as he stroked a hand up and down my back.

It was nice. And when I finally pulled back, not quite as ready to break down on him, he nodded. "There we go. Sorry if you didn't want a hug, but you looked like you needed one."

I waved the apology off. After all, he wasn't wrong; I *had* needed one. "I did, thanks. Now let's get inside so we don't get stormed on. I'll make dinner for both of us since you came rushing out to help."

Just as Thomas's hand cradled the base of my spine, gently turning me toward the house again, a noise cut through my disappointment.

A very familiar meowing.

Without a thought, I froze, spinning to face the noise as I squinted through still blurry vision. At first, I didn't see anything, and I deflated, but just as I prepared to turn around and head back, Thomas stepped forward with a frown.

"Hey, is *that* him? Up near the top of that tree?"

My head snapped up so fast, a sharp shot of pain slid up my neck, but I ignored it. Because sure enough, just near the top branches of the tree was Bello. His fur stood on end, distress clear as he clung to the branch as if his life depended on it.

Considering how much of a klutz he was, it very well might.

Air shoved from my lungs in a massive gust, relief hitting like a brick over my head as I nodded. "Yeah, that's him, but how do we—?"

Thomas cut me off, gently setting the box of things down and tugging on his jacket. I watched, jaw on the ground, as he put the well-worn leather over my things before stepping purposefully toward the tree.

Until I grabbed his arm.

"Is that safe for you?" The question blurted forward and he paused, surprised by my concern, before another smile twitched across his lips.

"Yeah, I'll be fine. Might get a bit scratched up but with any luck, your kitty will jump down on his own when he sees me coming," he answered, warm hand patting mine before gently taking it off his arm. Again, he turned to the tree, eyeing it for a minute before grabbing the lowest hanging branch and starting to climb.

My hand rose to clasp over my hammering heart, the sight of Thomas climbing the tree so *easily* squeezing something in my chest before I shoved it down.

Not. The. Time.

He was being nice and saving my cat; I shouldn't repay that by drooling over him. No matter how nice his butt looked in those jeans every time he stretched...

Ugh, dang it! Behave, Virginia!

Forcing my eyes away from his behind, I watched as he made it to Bello's level and reached an arm out. Instead of clawing at Thomas, like I both expected and dreaded, Bello did the last thing I thought he would.

He jumped right into Thomas's arms.

Bello hated most everyone aside from me, so to see him willingly jump to Thomas was honestly a monumental thing.

Maybe it was because he knew he needed help getting down, or maybe Thomas's magnetic air worked on more than just me. Whatever the case, I was glad for it as Thomas carefully made his way back down the tree until both feet were firmly planted on the ground again and I could finally breathe.

He smiled, scratching a hand behind Bello's ear before offering him to me. "Here ya go, one tired kitty ready for a nap."

Immediately, I took him, Bello giving a weak purr as he snuggled into my jacket. The low vibration soothed the last of my fear, a brief spell of dizziness hitting before another thunderous *CRACK* sounded, reminding me that we shouldn't be out here any longer than normal.

"Thank you so much for this. I didn't even see him up there," I said, trying to pick up the rest of my things with Bello still clasped to my chest.

Thomas bent, snagging his jacket and the box, before gesturing for me to lead on. "You're welcome. Now, let's get inside. It's going to pour soon and I doubt the kitty would be happy soaking wet."

Matching stride with Thomas, I finally felt my heart crawl out of my throat for the first time since I'd learned he got out. Forcing a slow breath to sweep aside the last of the shards of panic, I weakly teased, "Actually, Bello likes water. Shocked me when I found that out. It's the thunder he doesn't care for."

As proven by the tiny claws already digging into my clothes and chest. Poor Bello, he probably didn't sign up for all this adventure.

Thomas shot me an amazed look before he chuckled. "He'd be the first cat I ever met that enjoys it then."

Just as we made it into the house, another roll of thunder came before a torrent of rain hit next, tapping away at the roof as Thomas shot it a long look.

"Driving in that is going to suck."

Risking a glance out, I winced. Yeah, it would. People didn't know how to drive even without the rain. Which means I'd just have to be sure he didn't go out until it'd let up.

Gently setting Bello down after double-checking that the window was closed, I wrapped a hand around his arm–holy shit, my fingers didn't *fit* around his bicep!–and tugged him toward the kitchen.

"You should wait it out. I promised you dinner anyway and I'd be guilty if you got hurt in that mess," I said, watching the play of emotions on Thomas's face. At first, he looked ready to argue, but another well-timed CRACK cut him off.

He nodded, "I'll take you up on that, though I'll have to call Ma. She always worries when we don't update."

I hummed, already moving to gather the ingredients for dinner as I heard him talk with his mother.

"Hey, Ma. I got caught in the rain and I'll be back later."

He paused, listening before he huffed. "No, everything is fine, I just helped Virginia find her cat and she's making us dinner while we wait out the rain."

After a beat, he sputtered, lowering his voice in an attempt for me not to hear despite the fact we were in the same small kitchen.

"*No*, Mom. That isn't what this is. She's worried about me driving in that mess, nothing more and nothing less. Don't make it into anything it isn't—"

Whatever his mother said cut him off. I snuck a peak over my shoulder only to bite back a laugh at the crimson flush stretching all the way back to his ears. His hand pinched the bridge of his nose and he looked ready to combust from embarrassment.

What could she have possibly said to turn him that red?

As if in answer to my thoughts, he whispered just barely loud enough for me to hear.

"No, Mom, condoms are *not* necessary for this—"

Oh, *oh*. That's what she was saying.

Biting back a grin as a matching flush painted my cheeks, I kept my back to him as he continued. "I don't mean I wouldn't be safe in such a situation, Mother. I mean that now *isn't* that situation!"

Another few seconds passed before he let out a long sigh of defeat. "Yes, Mother. If we do wind up doing that, I will use protection, but that won't happen. Now please, drop this."

Apparently, his mother did because I heard him grumble a goodbye before hanging up. Keeping my stance and body language neutral, I pretended I didn't hear that as I asked, "Do you want tacos?"

He jumped a bit but answered, voice just a bit unsettled from his previous discussion. "Tacos are fine. Thanks."

I nodded, gesturing for him to take a seat when he shuffled in place, obviously uncertain where to sit. He was too cute. And teasing him was entirely too much fun.

Once he was seated, I heard the familiar patter of nails on the floor, barely turning in time to catch Thomas's noise of surprise as Bello hopped into his lap. He didn't hesitate to rub right up against

Thomas's throat either, his loud purr sounding through the air as I choked back a laugh.

"He really likes you, and that's an accomplishment. He hates everyone else he's met." Though, to be fair, that'd mostly been Steven, and now I knew why. Maybe Bello had a great sense of character.

He sure seemed to love Thomas.

Thankfully, Thomas took it in stride, hand stroking down the uneven fur without missing a beat as he shrugged. "There are plenty worse things in the world than approved by a cat. I'll take it as a compliment. Though I have to ask, Bello?"

Immediately, my cheeks flushed and I shrugged, looking away as I mumbled, "I don't care what others say; he *is* beautiful. He survived a horrible situation and still acts like the biggest cuddle bug to me. That makes him beautiful. Screw society's standards."

I could *feel* Thomas's eyes boring into me, the minutes ticking by slowly before finally, he made a noise of agreement. "You're right; he is. My father would approve of the name. I'm sure you noticed his accent; he used to live in Costa Rica, but he came to the states on holiday once and met Mom. The rest, as they say, is history."

Relaxing now that the topic shifted, I couldn't help but grin. "And seven boys later?"

Thomas nodded, "Yup. Mom definitely had her work cut out for her with all of us. Especially since Dad wasn't there most of the time. There's a good reason every single one of us respects her, and it's not just because we know she can whoop our behinds in a heartbeat no matter how old we get."

The image made my lips twitch up against my will. Somehow I could see Penelope doing just that, should her boys earn her ire. The woman may be smaller than them, but the sheer presence she had was immense.

Probably acquired from raising said boys and keeping them in line.

I didn't envy the woman for that, but seeing how close his family was? That I did envy.

Forcing aside the depressing thoughts, I finished the last of the meat for tacos and set up the tortillas, veggies, and cheese.

"She seems amazing. Now come on, dinner is ready, and I don't know how you eat your tacos."

He stood up, but instead of going to grab his food, he waited, watching me expectantly. When we stared at one another like owls for a minute, I tilted my head. "Aren't you going to grab some?"

After all, he must be hungry by now. Instead of doing that, though, he shook his head and nudged me toward it.

"Nope, not until you eat. Women and kids eat first, always. I'm a black hole, and I refuse to risk you not getting enough food."

I almost moved to argue, but something stopped me. It was sweet that he worried so much, not to mention it was a breath of fresh air to have someone *to* worry about me. He opened doors, pulled back chairs, and made sure I ate first.

Honestly, I hadn't met a single person like him, and every new thing I learned made me want to know him more.

A dangerous thing, but my usual skin-crawling fear wasn't present as I nodded and built my taco. Thomas wasn't a threat, at least not to me. Despite only knowing him a day, I knew that.

Threats didn't act like he did, doing things like rushing to my house to help me look for my cat and then climbing a tree when we found him. He was a nice guy, and it'd be nice to get to know him.

Flashes of Finn and Richard hit behind my eyes, and I couldn't help but wonder if they were the same way. They'd all been raised by the same woman, after all…

If so, I was glad. The world could use more men like the Hollimans.

Shaking that to the side, I sat down, watching as he split what was left of the meat and dressings into four massive tacos and took the chair across from me. The rest of the time passed in silence, both of us enjoying our food.

Just like in the car, this silence wasn't strained, and when we finally pushed back our plates without having broken it once, I knew I could get used to this.

The rain had let up at some point, but neither of us made a move to get up. There was no reason to rush, after all. It wasn't often I had company, and Thomas was quickly proving himself to be a good friend.

Maybe we could even make this a regular thing.

The thought sent jitters of excitement through me before I carefully tucked them away. *Friends*, I reminded myself. There was nothing wrong or weird with friends having dinner together. Definitely nothing to get nervous about.

Despite that, the wriggly feeling in my stomach stayed, and I mentally gave up.

Fine, whatever. It wasn't like it mattered whether or not I was just a *bit* happier to spend time with him. It wouldn't amount to anything so it could stay there.

Thomas broke me from my thoughts, his eyes trailing to the light drizzle outside as he did. "I should head out. Ma is probably hovering near the window, readying her interrogation. I'll…talk to you tomorrow?"

He hesitated on the last bit, uncertainty clear, and I nodded without thought. "Sure. My lunch is around noon so if you message me, I'll respond around that time."

I rose, following him to the door as Bello twined around his ankles. He shot the cat an amused glance, bending to stroke his ears before straightening again.

"Naomi is gonna be jealous of how much I'm petting your cat," he said, and without a thought, I grinned.

"I'll just have to give her lots of pets in return," I said, watching as Thomas snorted.

"Yeah, you'll never get rid of her then. Anyway, I'll head out. We can talk more about our hiking trip or something later. Have a nice night."

I nodded, watching through the window as he got back in his truck and left. Once he was out of sight, I dropped into a nearby chair and sighed.

"That was definitely not how I'd seen today going." Bello hopped into my lap, purring demandingly as my hand started carding through his fur.

After a minute, I couldn't help but smile. "But I can't say I don't like how things turned out." The smile dropped when I shot Bello with a stern glare. "That doesn't mean you're off the hook for getting out, though!"

I'd never understand how Bello could sulk, but somehow he did it...

Chapter 6

Pulling up to the fourth hiking trail Thomas and I had visited in the last month, I slid out of my car and swiped my brow absentmindedly.

The summer heat was no joke, and *this* time, I'd remembered to bring water.

My boots crunched across dirt and gravel as I made my way over to the front, where a few benches sat. Plenty of room to wait for Thomas there, and I could rest before the actual hike.

One bonus to our little outings, I was definitely staying fit. Taking a swig from my water, I eased back into the bench and sighed.

This hike had come at a great time. Work had been…trying yesterday. A new person in the town over had come to schedule therapy thanks to a stalker she'd had. Everything she said reminded me of my own situation so many years ago, and the memories were constantly under the surface now.

Not that my sleepless night helped with that at all.

I'd never been this on edge in my life, well, not since Steven was put away, and if it kept up much longer, I'd have to either get sleeping pills or see a therapist.

Or both.

Before the thoughts could run away with me to a place I really didn't want them to, the sound of tires on gravel dragged my head up. Thomas's truck parked next to mine, his frame folding out of it with ease. Only instead of heading for me, as usual, he moved to the passenger side and opened the door.

Two bodies blitzed out of the truck, one furry and one not.

Naomi hit the ground first, her tan and brown colors shining as she sat and waited for Thomas to give her an order. The German Shepherd was gorgeous, but my attention didn't stay on her for long.

No, the little boy at Thomas's side was *much* more fascinating.

Did he have a son? He'd never mentioned that or having a partner, but I guess it was possible.

Ignoring the sharp ache at the thought of him being taken, I waved as all three of them bounded over. The boy looked no older than five, his hair a shock of blonde in contrast to Thomas's darker locks, and piercing green eyes watched me with open wariness.

Once the trio stopped not far from me, I met Thomas's eyes and asked. "You didn't mention you had a son?"

Immediately, Thomas choked, his hand waving in the universal "no" motion, but before he could say anything–probably still trying to get air into his lungs, not saliva–the boy looked at me with a pout.

"He's not Daddy. He's Uncle Thomas."

Oh, okay, that made sense.

The pins pricking at my heart abated, though I wouldn't forget the pesky things had been there despite having *no reason to be.*

Shelving that for later thought, I leaned forward on my knees and nodded. "Sorry, I was just a bit surprised to see someone else with Thomas."

The boy seemed appeased with that, though Thomas raised a hand to scrub the back of his neck awkwardly. "Yeah, last-minute change of plans. My brother, Philip, had an emergency at work, and no one else was available. This is my nephew, Drew. Drew, this is my friend, Virginia."

Drew looked me over from his place hidden behind his uncle's legs, eyes sparking with curiosity even as he refused to leave his safe spot.

After a long minute, he mumbled, "Hi."

I gave him a smile before standing up and turning my focus to Naomi. "And this would be your faithful hound, I take it?"

Thomas's lips twitched, and he nodded. "Yup, she hasn't been too happy with me lately, going on hikes without her, so I figured it was time for an introduction." His eyes flashed to Drew, "Though I didn't plan on there being two."

Seeing the apology in his eyes, I waved it off.

"Eh, nothing wrong with meeting new people. Besides, this trail is supposed to be pretty easy, so it's perfect for a kid."

No sooner did the words leave my mouth than Drew finally moved out from behind Thomas to puff up in indignation.

"I'm not a kid; I'm almost six!"

I barely choked back the "aww" building at the back of my throat. I doubted Drew would appreciate it. Putting on a serious mask, I nodded. "Of course, my mistake. That's almost grown-up."

Drew beamed, obviously happy with that, as Thomas snorted. To his credit, though, he didn't say anything. Instead, he gestured to the trail, Naomi staying firmly at his side.

"Let's get this show on the road."

I followed easily, Drew breaking out of his shell the further in we got. By the time we reached halfway in, he was peppering me with questions I'd come to expect from kids.

"What's your favorite animal? Do you like snakes? I do. Are you Uncle Thomas's girlfriend? Will you two get married and have—?"

I nearly tripped over nothing at the sudden turn the questions took. Thomas reached over and cut his nephew off, a hot flush slapping across his cheeks as he cleared his throat.

"Drew, remember how we talked about some questions that aren't polite to ask?"

Drew screwed up his face in consideration before nodding, understanding dawning slowly as he looked at me. "Ooh. I did it again. Sorry."

The last bit was said more as an afterthought, but I forced a smile, ignoring the flutters taking residence in my stomach. "It's fine. Nothing wrong with asking a question. My favorite animal is actually a cat, specifically my cat Bello."

As if she understood, Naomi huffed, sending me a glare. I didn't bite back the chuckle in time as I patted her head. "Oh, don't start sulking. You're my favorite dog," I said, watching as she perked up, tail blurring behind her as I remembered the rest of Drew's questions.

Choosing my words carefully, I answered. "As for snakes, they're okay. I generally prefer to avoid them, but that's for safety's sake. I'm not your Uncle Thomas's girlfriend, though I am a friend of his who is a girl. I'm…not much one for dating and things like that."

I hesitated on the last bit. It was truthful but brought the topic just a tad too close to home.

Thankfully, Drew popped in with a sagely nod. "It's all ewwy. I don't want cooties. But Daddy said that'll change when I'm older. I don't want it to though. Girls are gross."

Usually, that was the case, but I wasn't about to get into asexuality with the kid, or aromantic for that matter. Instead, I said, "That's pretty normal, but you'll decide what you want as you get older."

Drew seemed to accept that, but the feeling of eyes boring into the side of my head made me look up. Thomas's mouth twisted down into a scowl, the sight pricking at the back of my neck as analyzing eyes swept down me.

Crud, I'd said too much and it'd caught his attention.

Before he could ask the questions all but drowning in his eyes, I pointed out toward a bright orange flower and called. "Hey, Drew, look. Isn't it pretty?"

Immediately, the boy bounded over to it, mouth open in wonder as I hastily followed, Thomas leveling me with an unimpressed expression at my not-at-all subtle subject change.

Well, too bad. I didn't feel like delving into my history and I'd happily use Drew as an excuse not to talk about it.

Things continued like that for a while, Thomas moving as if to bring something up and me pointing out a plant to Drew, but of course, all good things must come to an end.

"I gotta go potty," Drew said, pointing to the bathroom not far as we paused to rest. Thomas nodded, watching the only exit and entrance like a hawk as his nephew disappeared inside, Naomi following at his heel.

Before I could find something else to talk about, Thomas cut me off, eyes still not leaving the door.

"Listen, Virginia. If you don't want to talk about something, it's fine, I just have to know one thing," he said, the hair on my neck standing to attention as I reluctantly nodded him on. I didn't expect what he asked.

"Is anybody hurting you? I've noticed how tired you've been lately, and it's only seeming to get worse. Bruises are easy to hide, so if that lousy shmuck is hurting you, then just let me know and he won't be for long."

Oh, *oh*!

He thought I was being abused.

Warmth shuddered in my chest at the vicious protectiveness I could hear in his tone, but I shoved it down. He was a nice guy, of course he was concerned. That didn't mean anything and I needed to at least tell him I wasn't being abused.

Clearing my throat, I snuck a glance at the bathroom to ensure Drew was still out of earshot before answering lowly. "Thank you, but I'm not in an abusive relationship or a relationship at all. I haven't dated since I was a teen, and thanks to some events in the past, I never really want to."

Yeah, a stalker sure made dating difficult. At the time, I'd been too afraid for whoever I might date, and now just the thought made me uneasy.

Though, as I snuck a glance at Thomas, I had to admit–if only to myself–that the thought of dating *him* wasn't so daunting. He was respectful to a fault, never once raising his voice near me, and everything about him screamed safety.

But there was no way he'd want *me*. I came with too much baggage, and I knew that.

Better to not get my hopes up.

A hand covered mine on the table, snapping me out of my thoughts as Thomas gently squeezed, eyes still on the bathroom door as he spoke. "Is it too personal to ask about those 'events?' Or why did they make you swear off dating?"

Yes.

The word was on the tip of my tongue, but something burned in his eyes, even when they weren't pointed at me. Instinct told me I could say anything to Thomas, even the more damning parts of my history, and he wouldn't bat an eye.

I'd carried this for years without telling anyone and suddenly, for the first time, I wanted to share it.

Maybe not all of it to start, but...

Flipping my hand over and squeezing his back, I chose my words *very* carefully. "It's complicated but boils down to a man who didn't understand the words 'not interested.' He didn't manage to do anything permanent, but what he did left a foul taste in my mouth for any future attempts at dating."

All true, though definitely understated.

Thomas's jaw tensed hard enough for me to hear it crack, but he said nothing, mulling that over.

Then he threw me an entirely new curve ball.

Finally looking away from the door, he met my eyes, the sharp intensity sending sparks down my spine, and he asked. "I don't do well with things like this, but would you be interested in something...with me?"

Everything around us froze, my heart lunging up into my throat as I stared at him in open-mouthed shock. What was I supposed to say to that?

Well, the answer to his question was *yes,* I would be interested, but was it fair to him to start something when he didn't completely know what he was going into?

It wasn't, but the idea of having something with him, getting to see where this thing between us went…it was worth telling him just a bit more.

Sweat slicked my palm as I gripped his fingers, anchoring myself to the present as nerves threatened to start a riot in my stomach. Keeping my eyes firmly on our hands, I answered.

"I would, but trust me, you won't once you know more about me. There's a good reason I haven't dated in the past. I'm not fit for it. I don't handle it well when people try to make me do something, even if it's something small. I get snappy and nervous when I'm put on the spot, and that's not even getting into the thing that started it all."

The thing I really didn't want to talk about.

Instead of pulling away and agreeing, like I expected, Thomas tightened his grip and offered. "Good thing I won't be pressuring you on anything, then. You don't want to do something, then don't do it. Perfect example right now. You look like you're gearing up to talk about something you don't want to. Then don't."

He leaned just a bit more into my space, eyes softer as he continued. "If you're interested in this then we can talk later, set the boundaries. Tell me what you're comfortable or not comfortable with. You don't have to tell me *why* the boundaries are there for me to respect them."

And just like that, my heart melted into a puddle at my shoes.

I nodded, throat too tight to say anything. He didn't need me to, though. He gave another squeeze before a loud voice jarred us to the present.

"Are you two going to kiss?" Drew asked, his face open and curious as I tried not to choke on air. Okay, note to self, children can teleport.

I shot an uncertain look Thomas's way, only to relax when he answered. "We'll see. For now, let's head home. Grandma should be home by now and she wants to spend time with you too."

Drew lit up, past topic forgotten as he all but dragged Thomas and I back toward the car, Naomi loping happily at his side. I caught a flash of Thomas's smile as he buckled his nephew in and the upturn of his lips—and the warm look he sent my way—swept a round of butterflies into my stomach.

I never thought I'd try dating, not after all that happened with Steven, but maybe it wouldn't be so bad. At least, not if it was Thomas I was trying with.

Chapter 7

Dropping off Drew with Penelope took hardly any time at all, the woman too wrapped into her grandson to pay attention to us.

Which was a God send, in my case. She'd looked ready to shove Thomas and me in a room the last time we were here, and with my nerves already climbing the last thing I needed was to have those eyes on me.

We managed to get back out without being noticed, the silence between us crackling with tension until we got in our separate cars to drive to my house. The alone time let me pull in some much needed air and start putting the words together.

A relationship. What all could I do or not do in one?

He'd want to know that at least, which meant I had to figure it out. I'd spent so long avoiding even thinking of this that I was adrift in the proverbial ocean with no idea which way to turn for land.

I didn't mind physical touch. Thankfully, that hadn't been one of the issues I walked away from the entire Steven situation with. Judging by how nice holding his hand was, or being in his arms from the day he'd rescued Bello, I'd say I was *more* than happy to be cuddled with him.

But what about the more intimate things?

Having anyone see me naked was uncomfortable, not because I minded how I looked, but because I still remembered the pictures of me, sitting on my bed as if I'd put them there. Steven had taken them from outside my window with me none the wiser.

Every single picture was of me changing, though his final attack—and the one that'd doomed him—had been considerably more personal.

I hadn't even thought to close the drapes before hiding away in my room for some much-needed sexual tension relief.

A shudder rolled down my spine at the memory. I hadn't realized he was even there, watching.

Violation slid up my spine like a slimy snake, my stomach rolling even as I ruthlessly shoved it to the side. Yeah, being vulnerable and naked was going to be a hard one for me.

Maybe it'd be different with him, or maybe it wouldn't. Agonizing over it now wouldn't do any good.

My house came into sight in no time, and it was only then that I remembered that Naomi was with us. Bello hadn't had any bad experiences with dogs so far, but was now the time to introduce him to one?

I'd wanted to jump right into the conversation about boundaries and such, but…

Apparently, I wasn't the only one who thought of that because Thomas hesitated outside his truck with the door barely open. Once I moved to his side, he nodded to Naomi. "I could go home and drop her off, but she's well behaved around cats if you want to do an introduction."

Shooting a long look back at the house where Bello probably lounged, I made my decision.

"Let's try an introduction. If it goes badly, then drop her off, but if things go well, I wouldn't mind Naomi coming to visit with you whenever you have time," I offered.

Thomas was more at ease with his furry friend at his side. I'd noticed that today on our hike, and if it made him feel better to have her, then that was fine with me.

It was Bello's opinion we still had to see about.

Thomas nodded, opening the door and ordering Naomi to heel at his side. With that done, we moved to the house. Just as usual, the second the door opened, the sound of paws on wood came until Bello launched himself into my arms.

His usual purr of greeting froze along with every muscle in his body when he caught sight of Naomi. He didn't bolt or hiss though. Staying perfectly still in my arms, he just watched.

When nothing happened after a minute, I slowly crouched to be on the ground and stroked his head. "Easy, Bello. She's friendly."

He eyed the dog who hadn't moved once, but his fur thankfully stayed down. After a long minute, he hopped out of my arms to move closer. Thomas had Naomi lay down, something that Bello seemed to appreciate as he sauntered over to sniff the new addition.

Naomi's tail beat the ground, but otherwise, she stayed perfectly still. Another minute passed before finally, Bello rubbed himself against Naomi's nose, the dog sniffing him curiously. That must have been the signal because Thomas relaxed and let Naomi's leash go.

"They should be fine now. Naomi isn't one to get too excited, and Bello seems okay with her." With that, he stood up, watching as Bello curled into the dog's side and settled down for a nap.

At that, I snorted. "Apparently, his like of you extends to your dog." Which was a good thing since it made things easier for us, but it was still funny to see a cat and dog coexisting so easily.

Thomas hummed before intense eyes turned my way and I remembered what we were going to talk about before.

Right. Relationships, boundaries, and trauma. Important stuff, can't forget it.

Gesturing back to the living room, I cleared my throat. "Well, let's get this started."

He hummed, following behind me until we were both perched on the love seat, my stomach rolling with excitement and nerves.

Once seated, I grappled for the words to begin. I'd never done this before and now it was coming back to bite me. Thankfully, after a long minute of failing to find words, Thomas offered one of his hands, palm up, between us.

"Easy, Virginia. There's no set way of doing this. Just say what comes to mind. Things you don't like or things you do. I'm not going anywhere," he said, voice low and soothing. The tone rubbed over my frayed nerves like a balm and I released a small breath.

Giving him a smile, I tried to take his advice. "I'm glad you're not leaving because I'm a mess with words so this might take a bit."

He shrugged before settling further on the couch behind us. "I don't have to be anywhere today."

His hand was a warm weight, keeping me anchored to the present as I bit my lip and slowly started. "Well, I can say with confidence that I'm not comfortable with the more intimate things yet. Do you mind waiting a bit for those?"

Most men would have freaked, but Thomas only nodded. "Sure thing, can't say I'm the type to jump straight into bed either. Once we're both more comfortable in that way, we'll bring it back up. Deal?"

Tension eased out of my shoulders at that. Okay, one hurdle down and who knows how many more to go. I focused back on him and answered. "Deal. I don't mind touch, as long as you avoid the groin and chest areas under the clothes. Actually, aside from those, I *like* your touch so feel free to do that as often as you like."

Heat crawled up my cheeks as a wide smile curled his mouth, his fingers squeezing lightly around mine. "Perfect, because I can already tell that I'm going to love touching you. Your skin is soft and feels great." To punctuate that, he slid his thumb along my inner wrist, the light touch sending ticklish jitters up my arm.

Shaking it off before I could get distracted, I lightly swatted his side. "Don't start, we still have more talking to do, and it won't get done if you distract me."

He smirked, the edges of his lips twitching with the mirth I could see glowing in his eyes. "Sounds like a good distraction to me, but continue."

Giving him a warning look, I tried to think of anything else that'd be important. He already said I didn't need to tell him the reason behind the boundaries, but maybe I could say a bit. I'd probably explain more once we were further in, but for now, this would do.

"The boundaries won't last forever; if I'm honest, I don't even know if they're necessary. I've never done this so I'm not sure what I'm comfortable or not with, so we'll just have to see as we go?" I said, the last bit coming across as more of a question as Thomas nodded.

"Not a problem, I went into the military right out of school so I can't say I have a lot of experience with these things either. Let's play it by ear and see how it goes, all right?" he asked, some of the weight lifting off my shoulders at how easily the conversation was going.

"Yeah, that sounds fine. And I don't think there's anything else for now. Eventually, I'll tell you more about why I'm...like this, but for now, I just want to enjoy having you here," I said, watching as a dopey smile unfurled across Thomas's lips. His arm wiggled around my shoulders, waiting for permission–which I gave–before he tugged me into his side.

Warmth poured off him like a fountain, soaking through both our clothes as I tucked my chin up into his shoulder. This was nice, no beyond nice, and as his mouth brushed the top of my head, sending a spiral of gooey emotions I still had to get used to down through my gut, I all but melted into his side.

Eyeing the remote not far from us, I grabbed it before offering it up. "Want to watch a movie? I'll make dinner for both of us afterward."

His hum brushed my ear, the air sending a jolt of awareness down my spine before he took the remote and started flipping through the various options on my smart tv.

"Sure, though I'll help with dinner. I may look like a behemoth but Ma made sure every last one of us knew how to get around a kitchen," he said, a dash of humor at the mention of his height making my lips quirk up at the corners.

"Nothing wrong with being bigger than most people, though now that I think about it…" I trailed off, shifting to sit up fully against him as my legs curled against his thigh. I hadn't noticed before but, "I never realized how much smaller I am than you."

Even sitting down, he dwarfed me, his muscled frame eclipsing my much slighter one. Stealing a glance at our arms, I marveled at the difference. His were like thin tree trunks, my fingers itching to see if they were as dense as they looked, and mine–while not chicken bones– were laughably small in comparison.

Thomas looked at both of us, comparing us as well, before taking my hand and holding it out in front of us. Flexing his fingers out, he waited until I copied the movement before snorting. "You're right. Didn't notice until now. Guess it makes sense. I haven't met many women as big as me."

He curled his fingers down over mine, calloused grip firm but not too tight before he chuckled. "It's damn cute."

That'd usually be something to be indignant about, but the way he said it, the lightness to his tone, soothed any ruffled feathers before they could really rise. Besides, he was right. Looking at the almost comical size difference in our hands, it *was* cute.

And that wasn't a bad thing.

Cuddling just that much closer to his side, I leaned into him and hummed. "I'm fine with being cute as long as it's with you."

At that, he snorted. "Never thought I'd hear the word 'cute' used with me, but sure. If it makes you happy."

Oh, I couldn't just not say something about that.

Turning to face him, sliding my arms around his shoulders in an almost hug, I teased. "Excuse you, good sir, you are definitely cute, and I refuse to hear anything else about it. Especially when you wrinkle your nose-just like that!"

As if on cue, his nose twitched up, and I poked it playfully. "Cute."

He raised a brow, but instead of saying anything against it, one of his hands shifted to cup my thigh, and in my next heartbeat, he'd tugged me into his lap. A startled choke came before I landed sideways, legs on one side of him with his arm wrapped securely around my waist.

When he didn't move again after a minute, I got comfy against his chest and chuckled. "Wanted me closer? You could have just asked; I'm always happy for a cuddle."

To prove that, I dropped my head over his heart, the steady thump comforting as he went back to movie surfing. "Could have, but the noise you made was worth it."

Ah, so that's why he'd done it.

Before I could tease him about just what kind of noise I made, a furry bundle lunged up onto the couch, Naomi wiggling herself to be between the arm of the couch and Thomas's free side. The man grumbled but didn't complain once the dog had settled.

No, it was only when Bello hopped up to lie across both our laps that Thomas barked a laugh. "When did I become a pillow for all of you?"

His tone was teasing, so I shrugged, an impish grin curling my lips. "Well, I'm pretty sure Naomi got those privileges from the day you started working with her. Bello is a cat so he thinks anything he wants is his, and as for me..." I trailed off, moving as if to get up. "I could move if you don't want me here—"

The words cut off when he easily tugged me back, his arm tucking around me pointedly as he huffed. "You're the only one in this situation that was invited into my lap. Of course you're fine. The furry brats should be happy I like them so much, though."

I didn't bother arguing that, reaching over to stroke each animal's head in turn before cuddling back into Thomas's chest. "You're a big old softy. You can't hide it from me now. I've seen too much." I said, happy with the nose wrinkle he gave to that.

To his credit, he didn't bother arguing. Instead, he shrugged. "Eh, there are worse things to be known as. Besides, I'm still fully capable of handing someone their ass if they try something. As long as that doesn't change, I'm happy with this. Besides, if this is what's considered 'soft,' then I have no desire to be anything else."

To prove that point, he dropped another kiss against my head, the gentle pressure making me tip my chin up until our mouths hovered over barely a centimeter apart. Tension sparked like lightning as I nudged forward enough to brush against him. "You missed."

The words were barely a whisper, but he chuckled all the same. "Apparently, let me fix that."

The kiss was slow, lips brushing against mine as we got a feel for each other. It only took a second before his tongue peaked out, sliding along the seam of my mouth, and I opened instinctively. Like a drugging haze, my mind clouded, everything in the room fading to us as his hand wound into my hair and the other one stroked down my spine.

Warmth plied me from seemingly every angle, my eyes drifting shut under the deluge until we pulled away for air who knows how long later.

That was going to be dangerous. We'd barely kissed for a few minutes, and already, my body was waking up in a way it never had before. My fingers itched with the urge to trail across his chest, and only fisting them into his shirt stopped it.

Shifting to find a better spot on his lap, I froze when he hissed, rough hands gripping my hips and holding me still. I didn't have a chance to ask what was wrong before he gently set me back, pulling me just a bit out of his lap as he spoke.

"Easy on the wiggling. I'll behave myself, but that promise doesn't count if you do that," he said, and it was only then that I felt it.

Something was prodding me from his lap, something long and hard. Heat slapped across my cheeks at the realization of what it was, and in the same second, a shot of molten heat dropped straight down between my thighs.

Obviously, I couldn't get a good feel from this angle, but from what I could tell? He was huge.

Or maybe that was standard-sized for men, I guess I wouldn't know, but it *felt* huge, and the thought that it would eventually be going in me...

A mix of excitement, nerves, and earth-shaking lust rolled through me.

Carefully sliding to sit against his side again, forcing the hormone-drenched thoughts away, I leaned into him and hummed. "Sorry, didn't think about it."

His arm came back around me, tightening me into him as he shook his head. "Not a big thing, just didn't think you'd be comfortable being prodded like that."

I wasn't, at least not yet. Though if the mild warmth still pulsing in my groin was any indication, it might not be as long as I'd first thought before I was.

Shelving that for future consideration, I mumbled a thank you before cuddling back into him. Today had been a rollercoaster of epic proportions, but I wouldn't take any of it back. Things were off to a good start and, fingers crossed, it would stay that way.

I could hope. After everything that life had thrown my way to this point, maybe I was due some peace.

Chapter 8

I all but walked on air as I moved around my office, the familiar apple candle burning in the background offering a pleasant smell as I hummed my way through the work day.

I didn't have too many patients, thankfully, which meant I had time to float on my cloud nine between appointments all of today.

And now it was nearing the end of the day. My last appointment hadn't shown–apparently, there'd been a last-minute sitter issue, nothing drastic–which left me closing up early.

Tugging my phone out, I shot off a quick text to Thomas.

Last-minute cancellation, closing up early. Want to come over? – V

It'd become a habit after two weeks of dating to let him know when I was off work. More often than not, he'd make his way over, sometimes with Naomi and sometimes not.

Thinking of the last two weeks pulled a dreamy sigh from me.

Things have been perfect.

I'd never thought dating could be so much *fun*! It'd always seemed needlessly irritating before, but now I couldn't stop grinning at the thought of what Thomas and I would do later.

Just dinner and a movie, nothing massive, but I preferred it this way. We'd tried going out to a restaurant that wasn't Finn's, a fancy one, and it'd been a disaster.

Thomas didn't handle crowds well, and to be honest, neither did I. We barely made it past the appetizer before both of us were all but running for the door. After that, we'd agreed to keep the dinners to small diners or at home.

It also removed a lot of stress around it, which I appreciated.

I didn't care if where we went was some swanky place. All that mattered was that Thomas was there with me. Anything past that was negotiable.

Though if he chose to wear that button-up and tie to all of our dates, I *certainly* wouldn't complain.

And when I'd told him as such, he'd laughed long and loud enough to startle Bello in the next room over.

Despite the teasing that got me for the rest of the day, I noticed in our last few dates he had worn it again, even shooting me a knowing look whenever he caught me glancing his way.

So I liked a man in a sharp shirt and a tie, sue me.

Putting the last paper into the finished folder, I straightened my desk one last time before freezing when my phone vibrated on my butt. Tugging it out, I immediately smiled what was probably a giant and goofy grin.

The answer to that will never be no. I'll bring the dessert. <3 – T

It was a stupid thing, how my heart flipped in my chest and melted at that tiny heart, but I couldn't bring myself to care.

Of course when I moved to respond, my thumb hit the call button. Scrambling to stop it before it dialed, I winced when I wasn't quick enough.

Thomas picked up immediately, voice cheery and light.

"Couldn't resist hearing my voice?"

The teasing hint to his tone made my cheeks flush even as I mentally shrugged.

It wasn't like there was anything wrong with calling him after I was done working.

Keeping my hands busy with putting the last of my things away, I responded.

"Nope, though full disclosure, the call was an accident. Not to say hearing your voice is a bad thing—"

A resounding knock cut me off, the loud and sharp noise nearly making me jump out of my skin. Shooting a glance at the door, I bit back the urge to groan. Of course I had to have a walk-in today.

Pasting on a smile, I muttered into the phone while moving to answer it. "Our plans might get pushed back a bit, looks like I have a potential patient."

I vaguely heard Thomas's hum, but all noise faded into a dull buzz when I opened the door. "Hello, is there something I ca—?"

All the warmth from earlier drained out, ice taking its place as my fingers–which had previously been hovering over the end call button–went numb. Thomas's voice echoed from seemingly far away, drowned out by the rushing blood in my ears as I looked straight into Steven's eyes.

The eyes that were supposed to be in jail for stalking me.

"What are *you* doing here?"

Fear hid just under my tone, making it shakier than I'd like, but when I noticed the deranged glint to Steven's eyes, I shuddered. Air sucked into my lungs as I screamed, but Steven's hand lashed out, clamping over my mouth to stop any noise as he snapped up my phone and–without a word–hung up.

With a casual shrug, he tossed it across the room, ignoring the crack it made against the wall as he leveled a predatory smile my way. I ripped myself away from his hand, disgust at the touch flaring through my veins as I staggered back. My only exit was behind him, and he knew that, his steps slow and sure as he chuckled darkly.

"I see you've been cheating on me, and after I went through the trouble of getting out two years early for you." His voice all but dripped with sinister promise, the hair on my neck standing to attention as I desperately looked around for anything that'd work as a weapon.

Last time, he hadn't escalated to violence, but that was years ago, and I didn't trust that things hadn't changed. Besides, the look in his eyes, the way he raked them down my frame, I knew what he wanted, and I'd die before I gave it to him.

Lunging back to keep my desk between us, I glared with every ounce of anger in my body while hoping it masked my fear. He wasn't supposed to be here!

But he was, and I could wonder just why that was later.

"I didn't cheat on you because that would mean I'd ever *agreed* to be with you to begin with, which I didn't. You have no claim over me, and if I want to date, then I will, and you have no say in it," I said, chin tipping upward even as my stomach soured.

Technically he *had* kept me from dating these past few years, but not for the reason he thought. I definitely wouldn't be telling him that, though.

His smile dropped into a scowl, the hair on my neck standing up as he moved as if to go around the desk, my legs thankfully carrying me as I scurried to keep it between us. His eyes caught that, darkening slightly as he scoffed.

"Considering what I've seen you doing in your room, I'd say I'm more than a friend, and what better than a lover? I'd treat you right if you just stopped running." The words were slimy, leaving an almost physical trail in my skin as I shuddered.

"You'll never be anything but a stalker to me, *nothing*. You broke into my home multiple times, violated my privacy—" He cut me off, jaw tensing as he snarled.

"I wouldn't have had to do that if you'd just let me in! All I wanted was to care for you. Is that so bad?"

Without hesitation, I nodded. "Yes! Because I didn't agree to it. You were my patient, and even without the legal problems that comes with that, I don't like you that way. You have no right to me, and I refuse to give you one."

Before I could make a lunge for my phone, wherever it was now that he'd thrown it, he feinted one way, and when I lurched in the other he quickly changed directions and caught me around my waist.

Fear blitzed through my veins as I struggled against his hold, one of his arms holding mine to my sides as he shoved me against the sharp edge of my desk, his mouth leaning down to brush my ear.

"There, see? It's all so much easier when you just cooperate. I promise, it'll feel great, but if you keep fighting me…" He paused to bite *hard* into my neck, his flat teeth sending lightning pain through my skin. "Then I'm not going to bother being gentle at all."

Revulsion curdled my stomach as his mouth drifted away from the now pulsing bite mark, a trail of filth following every brush of his lips as I ramped up my attempts to get away. His arm around my waist stayed firm no matter how much I tried to wriggle free, his other hand trailing down to my jeans as my skin crawled.

I had to get away, had to!

His fingers slid underneath the waistband just as the door to my office slammed open. Steven spun around, still keeping his hold on me, and relief hit with the force of a wave at the sight of Thomas standing in the doorway.

He must have come running when Steven hung up, thank *God*.

My legs shook, unable to hold my weight from adrenaline and relief, as Steven tried to play the entire situation off.

"I'm having a bit of a moment with my girlfriend here. If you could leave?" His tone was perfectly annoyed, as one would be if we actually *had* been dating, but thankfully Thomas knew better.

His eyes flashed down to Steven's hold on my waist, his thumb now under the waistband as his other hand snapped up to cover my mouth so I couldn't object. When Thomas's eyes slid back to mine, I nearly flinched back at the pure wrath in them.

He didn't give Steven a chance to do or say anything, his body a blur as he lunged forward. In my next heartbeat, I was free, leaning against the desk as my legs threatened to drop out from under me, and Thomas had parked himself squarely between Steven and me.

Unfortunately, that also left the door behind Steven, and he didn't hesitate a second in using that escape once he realized Thomas wouldn't be moving.

He paused long enough to send a scathing glance my way and a hiss. "This isn't over."

Then he bolted, Thomas's muscles bunching as if to follow, only to stop with an uncertain look over his shoulder at me.

Whatever he saw, it made his decision for him.

Turning away from the door, he moved closer, only to pause a few feet away with his arms raised. Hesitance wafted off him in waves, and when I saw the worry in his eyes, afraid of putting himself where I didn't want him, the floodgates on my emotions broke.

Tears poured forward against my will, the fear from before draining out to leave an exhausted relief in its place as I threw myself into his chest.

That could have gone so much worse.

Even now, Steven's touch slid across my skin, the urge to scrub it raw growing by the minute as Thomas's arms came around me, offering a warm and solid shield against the world.

Later I'd cringe over how much of a mess I must look, but right now? I couldn't bring myself to care.

Crumbling into his chest, I let the adrenaline fade as the tears flowed. Thomas froze at first before his hands stroked up and down my back, his hold firm as he carefully rocked us in place.

By the time I had myself back under control a nasty headache pulsed at the corner of my temple, but I was almost clear-headed. Which meant I knew what we needed to do, no matter how much I didn't want to.

Looking up at Thomas, his eyes still dark with concern and anger, I spoke.

"We need to call the cops, and afterward, I need to tell you something."

Chapter 9

The cops showed up quickly, and from there, everything became a giant blur of sound and motion. Thomas stayed at my side for every minute of it, only leaving when the cops insisted that I give my statement and tell them about my history with Steven.

A part of me was glad Thomas hadn't been in the room for that. He deserved to learn this from me, not as second-hand knowledge while I told someone else.

On the other hand, that meant I had to talk about this twice.

Exhaustion chewed at the edges of my mind, but I forced it back, listening to the cop as kind eyes with plentiful crows feet watched me with concern as I walked him to the door to leave.

"I'll make sure to let the others know to keep an eye out for him. I advise getting a restraining order if you don't already have one. He has a history with you, and he definitely isn't going to drop it now."

I nodded numbly, barely managing to mutter through my numb haze. "I have one against him already. He ignored it the first time. That's part of how he ended up in jail." That and the many threats he gave, not to mention breaking and entering...

I shuddered at the memory. Thomas's arm came around my shoulders, anchoring me to the present as the cop nodded, sympathy clear in his eyes as he did.

"I'll note that down too. Anytime he tries to contact you or leaves any messages, give us a call. Every bit of evidence we get against him is more we can hopefully use to put him back in jail and *keep* him there," he said, the words sharp with an undercurrent of steel.

I was too far in my own head to respond, everything that's happened coming down to push against me at once as my head spun from all the information.

Steven was back out, *legally*.

Steven was after me again and knew where I lived despite me moving states away.

Steven wasn't content with messages and breaking into my house now.

Steven was becoming even *more* unhinged, and if today's attack was any indication? The next time he caught me unaware, I would need a weapon of some sort.

And with that sobering thought, I lurched out from under Thomas's arm and barely made it to the garbage can in time to lose my lunch.

Dimly, I heard the cops file out, leaving just Thomas and me again, before the man himself carefully sat next to me, his hand patting my back in an awkward attempt at comfort.

I couldn't blame him. I wouldn't be doing any better in his position.

Leaning into the touch, I pulled back when the last heave rocked my stomach and acid burned my tongue. Swallowing back as much of it as I could, I took a deep breath and muttered, "Sorry you have to deal with this."

Thomas shook his head, hand gently guiding me over until I sat curled against his chest with my head pressed up into his throat before he rumbled. "Nothing to apologize for. I only wish I'd gotten a hold of that fuck before he ran. Then you wouldn't have to worry about any of this. But wishing doesn't do anything, so instead, how about we get you home to relax? I'd say you've more than earned it, and I'm sure Bello would be more than happy to cuddle you while I get dinner ready."

Nothing sounded better at the moment than that.

Leaning all of my weight against him, I followed Thomas as he led me to his car. I only glanced at mine once before he shook his head. "Don't. You're in no state to be driving. If you want, we can come back for it later or tomorrow. Heck, I could even ask one of my brothers to swing by and pick it up and drop it off at your place. Whichever you prefer."

Holding out one of my hands, I watched it tremble and shake before mentally giving in. He was right, driving like this was begging for an accident, and I definitely didn't need that on top of everything else today.

I nodded, letting him help me into the passenger seat as the warmth of the interior chased away the chill biting my bones.

Things were far from okay, but with Thomas here, it was at least starting to look up. I still had to worry about Steven–he found me at work; did that mean he knew where I live now too?–but with the scent of Thomas all around me, I let the worries fade back.

I could focus on them later when I felt less like I'd been yanked through the wringer. Besides, I still wasn't done yet. Once we got back to the house, I'd need to explain more about Steven, an exhausting conversation, to be sure, but a necessary one.

The drive to my house was shorter than I remember it being, but I didn't dwell on it. Instead, I gratefully accepted the arm Thomas offered as we headed inside. Bello greeted me as always, his little body a massive bundle of fur and purring, and the familiarity sank through me like liquid heat.

It was only when we were both seated on the couch, Bello still parked in my lap, that I finally faced the conversation I knew was coming.

Turning just enough to face Thomas, the man once again sitting at my side just like we had weeks ago when we'd started dating, I took a deep breath and started.

"This topic isn't easy, and I'd appreciate you not interrupting. I might not be able to get through it if you do," I said, eyes flitting between Thomas and Bello.

Thomas nodded, but before I could start, his hand trailed over mine, giving it a gentle squeeze. "You don't have to tell me anything. Keep that in mind."

I know I didn't, but he needed to know this, and maybe it was time I got this out.

Giving him a small smile, I pushed on. "Thanks, but this is important, and now with him back, with Steven back, it's important you know what's going on."

Again, he nodded, only this time he leaned back into the couch and lifted his arm in offering. I sank into his side with relish, a blanket of safety settling over me when he tucked me against him again.

Pulling from the reassuring weight around me, I started back at the beginning.

"Steven is the man from earlier, and years ago, he was put away for stalking me. Apparently, they let him out early because he wasn't supposed to be free for at least two more years…" I trailed off, the idea that anyone would *allow* him back out without even thinking to notify me sending hot wrath through my veins.

He'd stalked me relentlessly, broken into my home, and threatened me. Shouldn't that be enough to warrant at least a phone call? Nothing major, just a warning like "Hey, we let out your stalker who has a history of mental instability. Cheers!" I wasn't asking for the world here…

Forcing back the anger, I looked over to Thomas. His face was a mask of carefully controlled rage hidden poorly by concern. It didn't surprise me, though, he was the sort to be protective over those he cared about, and now I fell under that category.

Patting his chest, practically feeling the bloodlust swirling under his skin, I continued. "I'm sure you can see where this is going. Steven stalked me for months, ignoring the fact that I had no interest in him. Originally, he was one of my patients, and I used that as an excuse to turn away his advances. He stopped coming to therapy in an attempt to circumvent that. When I continued to refuse, he started escalating."

Escalating, that sounded so tame. The word didn't even begin to explain the terror of coming home to find the photos he'd taken strewn over my bed. Thankfully, he'd left Bello alone, but the fact he'd even been in my house without my permission, even going through my underwear drawer at one point, left my skin feeling itchy with invisible filth I couldn't get rid of.

Curling closer to Thomas on instinct, his towering frame offering comfort I desperately needed, I forced the rest out. "It started as just notes left at my work or on my doorstep. Unsettling, but easy to ignore. Then the notes started getting more explicit, and pictures started showing up with them. Pictures of me in my room, undressing…"

I hesitated, the memories sweeping a cold wind through me. Even now, the violation was strong, sitting just under my skin as if it'd never left.

Thomas's arm tightened around me, but he said nothing, keeping in mind my request not to interrupt. Tipping my chin back to give him a tiny smile, I finished the last of it.

"Eventually, it got worse to the point he started leaving them inside my room after I'd locked the door and left for work. I got a restraining order, but he ignored it. Unfortunately, there was no evidence that it was *him* leaving the photos and notes, so the cops couldn't do anything about it. Until the last batch he left."

My stomach soured, but I pushed on. Just a little more and I'd never have to talk about this again.

"I came back from work to find pictures of me, naked and... mid-orgasm. He'd taken them from the window in my room, and alongside the pictures, he'd gone through my underwear drawer. One of my favorite pairs was on my bed with the photos, and he'd completely covered it with *him*."

I didn't specify and Thomas didn't need me to. His low hiss cleaved through the air, his jaw creaking loudly next to my ear as he bit back the urge to snarl. The urge to get up and hunt Steven down was all but drifting off him in waves, and I patted his chest absentmindedly. "I know. But on the bright side, that's what gave the cops the evidence they needed. DNA match. They put him away and now he's back."

And if earlier was any hint, he wouldn't be content with just dirtying my underwear and scaring me. No, the stakes were higher now, and even the idea of what could have happened soured my stomach like week-old milk.

All but burrowing into Thomas's chest to hide from it all, I relished in the safety of his arms as he shifted us. Lying back on the couch, he reclined before opening his arms in offering. I didn't hesitate, sinking down to use him as a mattress, Bello jumping to the floor and running off as he was known to do.

My nose pressed into his neck, one of my hands coming to rest over his heart as we settled further into the couch. Even from here, I could hear the steady thrum of his pulse, the sound helping to ease the last of my lingering discomfort from the previous topic.

At first, he didn't say anything, seeming content with the quiet of the moment, but after a long few minutes of just breathing one another in, he spoke.

"If I ever meet him again, he won't be walking away from it. I promise you that. Fuck, for anyone to do such a thing! And to you!" His tone rumbled with deadly warning, and I inched closer in response. It was nice, having someone be just as repulsed as I was.

There were people in the courtroom, especially Steven's slimy lawyer, who'd tried to insist that it was okay, that it was somehow *my* fault for everything because I turned Steven down in the first place.

Thankfully, the judge hadn't been impressed, but the fact someone could even try to spin it like that was horrific.

"I know, and while we're on this topic, I'm probably not going to be comfortable with most PDA. After those pictures…I just don't like the idea of anyone seeing my private moments, our private moments."

Thomas had never tried kissing me in public in the past few weeks and it was a good thing, I would have refused and probably hurt his feelings in doing so.

But the idea of anyone other than us being privy to those minutes made my skin crawl.

Thomas's hand stroked down my back, his other one drifting to my chin to gently pull it up and meet my eyes again.

"That's perfectly fine. I got the vibe that you preferred it that way, and it's why I didn't try anything whenever we were out. It's okay to be uncomfortable with things others are fine with. All I care about is you," he said, eyes locked on me as his words all but vibrated with the force he put behind them.

Tension eased from my shoulders as I nodded, beyond relieved he hadn't taken that the wrong way. I guess I shouldn't have been surprised. After all, this was *Thomas*. Not once had he pressured me in our relationship, and this was no different.

Inching forward to peck his lips, I smiled, the small stretch feeling more genuine than it had just a few minutes ago. "I feel the same about you."

The day we'd gone to the fancy restaurant had been agony for more than just one reason. Seeing how uncomfortable he'd been, nearly jumping out of his skin anytime someone entered through the door that was behind him–horrible seating choice on the server's part–had been a major part of what led to me hustling us out the door so quickly.

Just like he hated seeing me uncomfortable, I was the same with him.

Silence passed between us after that, the quiet comforting as I soaked in the fact that someone else knew the entire truth of Steven and the mess he'd made. It was nice, finally having someone in my corner who wasn't Bello.

Speaking of Bello, I should probably feed him. It was getting late, and honestly, it was amazing he hadn't come demanding food yet.

As if in response to my thoughts, the familiar furry body jumped onto my back, paws kneading into my back as he shoved his entire head against my neck and meowed demandingly.

Biting back a laugh at the hairs tickling my neck, I reached back to stroke his head. "All right, all right. I got it; no more lazing on the sofa for Mommy. You need food, and I'm on it."

Moving to get up, I stopped short when Thomas stood as well. When he caught my surprised expression—I didn't have time to hide it—he smiled.

"I told you I'd make dinner, and since you're already up and moving for Bello, there's no point in me sitting here with my thumbs up my a—" He cut himself off, a sheepish smile curling his lips as he shrugged. "Well, you know what I mean."

One of these days, he'd realize I didn't mind him cursing around me, but a smattering of warmth glowed inside my chest all the same. It came from a place of respect so I could appreciate it.

Giving his hand a squeeze, I tugged him down for a quick kiss on the cheek before heading to feed Bello. "You don't have to, but because I know you're going to ignore that, thank you. I appreciate both the help and the company."

I didn't wait for his reply, though I did catch a glimpse over my shoulder before disappearing around the corner. One of his hands was raised to cup the cheek I'd kissed, a smile stretching his lips as his eyes melted in what I could only label adoration.

Whatever it was, it sent my heart into a series of spins to see it. Focusing on the present and my demanding cat, I put the look and its owner to the side for now.

Besides, I'd have plenty of time to see it again, I was sure. No need to rush it now.

Chapter 10

The store was a bustling hive of activity, sounds, and colors blurring together as I deftly weaved through the crowds.

I loved the holidays, but I could definitely do without all the people and their last-minute shopping.

Thomas had taken one look at the parking lot before reluctantly admitting he should stay in the car. No surprise there. With this many people, he would have been constantly on edge. He'd mentioned once how slowly his adjustment back into civilian life was going–his frustration with the fact clear even without him saying so–and I did my best to comfort him.

Healing wasn't easy, quick, or linear. As I knew better than most.

To be honest, I'm proud he even told me he needed to stay outside. He came off as the sort to try to shove his way through any discomfort despite the damage it inevitably did to him. I'd have to make sure he knew I appreciated that later.

Sweeping a glance around the store again, I finally caught sight of what I'd been looking for. The "adult" aisle. From one end to the other were various drinking games, strip poker boxes, and condoms. I came here for the latter, but the colorful boxes caught my attention.

Thomas and I hadn't done anything in that regard aside from kissing and some *very* heavy petting, but with the tension crackling between us, it was only a matter of time. Having a box of condoms was a must, but maybe I could get a game to go with it?

Slowly strolling down the options, I ignored the drinking ones—Thomas's warning that alcohol didn't agree with him still at the forefront of my mind—and went straight to the other end of the aisle.

There were less of them, not surprisingly, and it made perusing the selection easier. One box caught my attention, the familiar mat and colored circles on the front spiking confusion through my veins.

What was Twister doing in this section?

It was only when I picked it up that I realized why it was here. It was *shower* Twister.

Heat licked up my cheeks before I hastily put it back. It sounded kind of fun but with my balance, I'd kill both of us by accident.

Glancing at the box next to it, I perused the wooden building blocks curiously. How did one make *building blocks* into an adult game?

Apparently, the answer was by putting naughty dares on them. It was built like Jenga, but every block you removed, you had to do. Reading some of the dares on the box, I swallowed hard around my suddenly dry throat.

That…had possibilities.

Putting it in the cart, I continued looking, half embarrassed and half fascinated. I'd almost made it to the end of the aisle—my cheeks ablaze by that point—when I saw it. A simple set of dice.

There were four of them in the set, each looking fairly innocent until you looked closer at the illustrations on the biggest die.

One of them was covered in words like: blow, suck, and kiss. Another had body parts on each side, a no-brainer what it was for, and the last two dice?

That's where things got *really* fun.

Each of them had twenty sides, and every single one of them had a tiny picture of a sexual position. I couldn't see most of them in the package, but from what I could see, they got pretty intense.

My thighs twinged at some of the positions even as the urge to buy it rose. I wasn't nearly flexible enough for these, but they looked fun.

Just as I went to throw them in the cart, damn the consequences to my thighs later, a bottle caught my attention. It was paint, *edible* paint, and immediately dozens of images flashed through my mind for what I could do with that.

No flexibility required *and* I could explore Thomas to my heart's content. A win-win.

Without hesitation, I threw a few different colors into the cart and made for the check-out. I didn't know when I'd be using them, but even having these things made giddiness shoot through me like lightning. I'd never thought I was the sort to buy naughty couple games, but I guess you learn something new every day.

The checkout lines were packed, to my dread, but I took up a spot at the back of the line and waited my turn. Or, I tried to.

Apparently, I'd looked too cozy minding my own business.

The man in front of me turned, something about the glint to his eyes making my skin crawl, and when he opened his mouth to talk, it was accompanied by a disgusting leer.

"Interesting selection you've got there." He gestured down to the games I hadn't thought of covering. Damn it; I should have. I wouldn't have to deal with this otherwise.

Setting aside my frustration with myself, I looked straight ahead and said nothing. I just wanted to get everything and leave, not deal with this slime.

Of course, he didn't like that.

Stepping into my line of sight, his smile twitched down a bit as he huffed. "Jeez, no need to act like such an ice queen. With that attitude, it wouldn't surprise me if you didn't have anyone but yourself to play those games with. Unless the unlucky shmuck is around here too?"

He shot a glance behind me meaningfully, and I had to resist the urge to tell him that yes, I did have a boyfriend, and he was nearby. Thomas was outside, and while I could send him a text to come in to help me with this, I wouldn't want to make him uncomfortable with the crowds that only seemed to be getting worse.

So I tightened my jaw and stood my ground. "This is none of your business and I'd appreciate you leaving me alone."

My voice was sharp and clear, carrying to the other people in line as people turned to stare. Some whispered, others rolled their eyes, and one man eyed the slime as if ready to step in at a moment's notice.

If it came down to that, I'd thank him. Focusing on the slime, who was now *not* happy with the attention, I instinctively stepped back as he leaned forward onto my cart. "No need to be so uptight. I was just offering to fix that problem for you. You obviously don't have a boyfriend with an attitude like that and I could help you pull that stick out of your ass."

Did people really think that *this* was how you flirted?

Before I could rip into him with every scathing word in my mental dictionary—most of which would woefully go over his head since they were over three syllables—a voice from behind me cut my response off.

"Get out of here, Jake. Before her boyfriend comes in for no other reason than to hand you your ass."

Turning to the new voice, I paused at the woman now glaring down Jake. She was shorter than me by a few inches, medium blonde waves pulled back into a bun, and icy blue eyes practically dared Jake to continue.

He took that dare.

Turning to face her now, he sneered. "Oh, like you're one to talk about boyfriends. Hell, the entire town knows that you fucked over the deputy when you were teens. Poor bastard, would hate to be in his shoes with some harpy who broke things off with *no* reason. What was

112

it, princess? Was he not high class enough for you? Or did he just suck in bed and you wanted better?"

The woman went deathly pale, her glare dropping as an old pain ripped through her eyes. "It was nothing like that…" Her words were hardly a whisper, and every syllable dripped with pain.

Before I could jump back in—or say fuck it and call Thomas—something about what he said clicked.

The deputy was *Richard*.

I took in the woman again through a different lens. So this was the woman who'd left him, left that hurt in his eyes. But…the more I looked her over, saw the matching pain blue orbs, the less it made sense.

I'd expected Scarlet to be some kind of uppity, drama-loving woman. Maybe one who'd spread rumors about Richard after breaking his heart and leaving, but this woman wasn't that.

She'd stepped in to stop Jake from bothering me when she didn't have to do that, and if she didn't care about Richard, *why* did she look so hurt now?

Apparently, Jake caught my wide-eyed understanding because he snorted. "Didn't realize who was coming to your defense, did you? Well, now you do."

Scarlet flinched, mouth tugging down into a scowl as the momentary vulnerability faded away, a steely shield coming up in its place. "Yeah, now she knows. But that doesn't matter because you're bothering her. Now *leave* before I get the store security."

"That won't be necessary because if he doesn't mind his own business, *I'll* escort him out."

I spun around, surprised to see Thomas looming over Jake with a ferocious glare. Did he have some kind of sixth sense for when I needed help? I wouldn't complain if that was the case. It certainly came in handy now.

Jake swallowed hard, looking Thomas up and down before backing away with his hands raised. "Easy man, if I'd known she was yours, I wouldn't have tried anything."

Thomas scoffed at that, moving to throw an arm around my shoulders as he did. "It doesn't matter who she's dating. You shouldn't bother *any* woman like that."

It was kind of funny watching Jake face forward and do his best to pretend none of us existed. Shaking that to the side, I leaned against Thomas and sighed. "Thank you, and sorry. I was trying not to get you involved since it's busy today."

He shook his head. "I was already hovering at the entrance waiting for you. Got the feeling something was going down, and then I caught a glimpse of him bothering you. It'll never be so busy that I won't step in to stop slimes like that."

And I appreciated it.

Soaking in the warmth drifting off his side, I remembered Scarlet a minute later and turned back to her. "Thank you for trying to help with him."

She froze, eyes wide as if expecting me to rip into her. And maybe she did. This town wasn't big, and everyone adored Richard, from what I'd seen. Whether it was the women who took him to bed or the little old ladies he periodically wound up chatting with while getting their cats out of trees.

For her to be the one who'd hurt him and for everyone to *know* that? The town probably was far from friendly with her.

Which brought up more questions than I knew what to do with. Why did she look so hurt when Jake brought up Richard? Why would she stay in this town even after she became a pariah?

I wouldn't be getting any answers either, at least not today.

Scarlet nodded, though when her eyes trailed up to Thomas, she flinched and moved to back away. "It's nothing, my pleasure. Now I need to—"

She didn't make it three steps before Thomas spoke, voice cutting through the air like a whip. "Stop."

She did, shoulders tensing into a tight line as she froze. "Why?"

Her question was quiet, resigned. As if she knew this particular conversation was unavoidable but that didn't mean she liked it anymore.

Stealing a glance up at Thomas, I noted his expression. Confusion and determination, an odd mix, but it made more sense when he spoke.

"Because I need an answer from you, and it's long overdue."

Scarlet twitched and for the briefest second I thought she'd bolt, but instead—after a long minute—she turned and pulled her cart in behind us with a nod.

"Fine, I guess I owe you that much."

Thomas shook his head. "No, you owe *Richard* that much, but since you won't tell him anything, I'll have to stand in and play relay. Now, what the hell happened while I was gone, Scarlet? When I left, you two were making calf eyes, and *you* were talking about marrying him, how many babies you guys would have, the whole enchilada. What changed?"

I watched as she looked away, the pain from before coming back as she tried to find the words. "Everything changed, but I can't tell you much. My father—"

She cut herself off, but not quick enough. Thomas's eyes narrowed. "Your father. The same one that's hated our family since the day his martial arts studio closed down. Your father who blamed our family as a whole for that because we owned his only competition?"

Slowly, the pieces were starting to click together, and the fractured picture they made soured my stomach. Scarlet hadn't seemed the type to shatter someone's heart for no reason, and now? I was starting to get a hunch for just why she did it.

Scarlet nodded, voice barely above a whisper as she continued. "Look, I *can't* tell you anything, all right? I can't tell you. I can't tell Richard, no one. I want to, oh my God, do I want to, but it's too dangerous—" She cut herself off, realizing a second too late what she'd said.

Thomas's eyes darkened to that. "Dangerous? You got someone *threatening* you over this shit?"

She didn't answer, jaw tight. Instead, she shook her head. "Of course I don't. But please, stop asking me things. I can't help but answer them, and I can't afford this. No, I didn't break things off with Richard because I wanted to, but that's all I can say. Take it or leave it."

Then she turned, hustling away. Thomas let her go without another word, his eyes following with the intensity of a hawk. Once she was out of sight, I cleared my throat and muttered. "She isn't what I expected after hearing about her."

He snorted, "No, she wouldn't be. I remember first getting the call from Ma when Scarlet broke things off. I've known that woman since we were young and I never expected her to do that. Especially as suddenly as she did. I always thought there was more to it, but with her refusal to talk until now…"

It was impossible to prove, and dragging up old memories wasn't a great way to start any day. Richard had obviously been hurt, anyone with eyes could see that, and he probably wouldn't take kindly to the topic being brought up.

Thomas shook his head, pulling us back to the present as we moved up to the cashier. "I have a lot to think about, especially that 'dangerous' bit. But for now, don't say anything to anyone about this, all right? Let's just focus on getting home. I'll mention it to Richard once I've got it all straight."

I nodded, not wanting to step into family drama. It was only after we'd left the building that he noticed the second bag of purchases.

"What are the paint and Jenga blocks for?"

Heat crawled up my cheeks as we climbed into his truck. Was now really the right time to mention them? Things still felt a bit charged from what happened in the store…

But I wanted to show him. I wanted to see his reaction to them, knowing *I* bought them. So, I handed over the bag and said, "Look closer."

He raised a brow, the stormy scowl curling his lips fading as he took it and picked up the blocks.

Only to freeze after a minute, his eyes sliding to the edible paint as understanding sparked and liquid heat warmed his eyes. Very slowly, he looked over at me, dozens of promises hidden behind his eyes as he cleared his throat.

"Do you want to use these tonight or was this a plan for the future kind of thing?" His voice was level, though anticipation leaked through.

To be honest, I'd meant for them to be later, but now that the images of what we could do were planted, I wanted to see them all the way through.

I wanted to feel him like that, and I didn't want to wait anymore.

Nerves buzzed in my ears as I took a breath to clear them and responded. "Either or, though if you aren't working with Helena today, I wouldn't mind heading home to break them open."

The bag dropped in my lap the next heartbeat, his fingers lingering over my covered thigh as he did. Tingles swept out like a wave from the touch, spreading further south when he growled.

"I'm not working today, and even if I had been, after that, I wouldn't be."

Sensual promise oozed from his tone, and instinctively, my thighs clenched together. We were doing this, and the closer we inched toward my house, the more excitement strafed my veins.

Even if we didn't wind up going the full way, something told me it was going to be amazing.

Chapter 11

The second the tires stopped in my driveway Thomas and I were moving for the house, the bag clutched in my hand. On entering, I noticed Bello lay sprawled in the sun, opening an eye in greeting before going back to his soak.

Good, that meant we wouldn't have to worry about curious kitties poking their noses in.

Once we stood outside my room, I glanced at the bag and spoke. "Do you want to start with the body paint or the blocks?"

To be honest, I wanted to touch him and every second I couldn't do that stretched on like a year. The blocks would be fun, but the idea of waiting for what I now knew was offered was torturous. Apparently, Thomas agreed because he took the bag, removed the paint, and handed it over.

Sharp eyes stayed locked on me as he spoke. "I'm too high strung for the blocks. We can do those later."

I didn't understand the meaning behind 'high strung' until he gestured down, my eyes trailing over the prominent bulge pressing against his jeans.

Oh. Okay, yeah, that made sense.

Nodding dumbly, I grabbed the other bottles of paint and nudged open the door to my room. He followed, carefully shutting it behind us, and with the soft *click* of the door, the intimacy of the room rose up.

Before I could start stripping, though, the window caught my attention and a chill slid up my spine. Setting the paint down on the nightstand, I inched over to it and glanced out.

Nothing.

But then again, I hadn't noticed Steven the first time either...

My previous arousal and excitement turned to ash, but before I could say anything, Thomas moved to my side. Some of the fire behind his eyes had faded, a softer understanding taking its place as he eyed the window.

"I could push something in front of it if you wanted?"

The offer took me off guard, head snapping up to stare at Thomas. When he met my eyes, he shrugged.

"You're not comfortable doing things where others *might* see, and thanks to that f—, that slime, you don't feel safe in here either. Pushing something in front of the window isn't exactly a difficult thing, and if it makes you feel safer, then I'm game."

I was going to squirt tears if he wasn't careful.

Warmth ballooned out in my chest at his non-judgmental tone, threatening to suffocate me from it as I nodded and stepped to the side to give him room. The window wasn't a big one, thankfully, and in hardly five minutes, he'd moved my bookcase in front of it.

Thomas stepped back, glancing to me for approval that I gave with a nod, fighting to swallow past the knot in my throat. I should have expected something like this, Thomas was *exactly* the kind of sweetheart to do this, but I hadn't, and now I was drowning in the emotions that came with it.

Without thinking, I wrapped my arms around his waist and buried my face in his chest; the warmth wrapped tightly around my heart pulsing in time with its beating as his arms wound around me. After a few seconds of soaking it in, I pulled back, noted his confused expression, and kissed his chin.

"You're amazing, and you're mine."

That was all the explanation he was getting, but if the way his eyes softened was any indication, he didn't need anymore.

His lips twitched up before he dropped, mouth trailing over mine in the lightest brush of lips. Sucking my lower lip between his teeth, he scraped lightly before letting go.

"And you're gorgeous and mine. We could do this all day–and trust me, that sounds like a good way of spending my time–but right now, there are other things I'd prefer to be doing." He paused, bending to nip the shell of my ear before breathing the rest. "Namely, you."

Hormones surged up in response, shouting their resounding agreement, and I nodded as well. "We can come back to this later, for now…" I trailed off, intertwining our fingers as I dragged him back to the bed. The paint sat in easy reach as I hovered near the edge. Staring up at him, I fiddled with one of the bottles and offered it.

"Do you want to go first, or should I?"

I'd never done anything like this before, but the idea of drawing patterns across his chest–and lower–before licking them off was a *damn* good thought. But he shook his head, palm gently pressing me back onto the bed as he did.

"You, at least this time. I'm ready to pop as it is, you put that pretty mouth on me, and it's gonna be over before we can even start. If you want to return the favor we can do that later," he said, and again my eyes dropped to his groin, where his length pressed valiantly against the jean.

I'd hold him to that.

Inching back to rest in the middle of the bed, nerves starting to peak out again, I forced my eyes to stay on him as I asked, "How do we do this?"

A slow smile stretched his lips, his movements graceful as he climbed on the bed and hovered over me. Once our mouths were barely an inch apart, he hummed. "However you want. You need to stop, you say so and it all ends. Got it?"

I nodded, leaning back into the bed as strong hands cupped my jaw before slowly sliding downward. When they rested on my hips, fingers hooking gently into the fabric of my shirt, he paused, waiting for permission.

I gave it, biting my lip as he slid the fabric up and over my head. A chill slid across the now bared skin, only my black bra covering my upper half as he shuddered above me.

"Fucking gorgeous." He growled, for once not apologizing for the curse as his mouth dropped to slide a kiss down my chest, trailing to my stomach before stopping at the waistband of my pants.

It didn't take him long to get rid of those too, his eyes trekking down my frame and drinking every inch in like a man dying of thirst would stare at a glass of water.

Calloused fingers wiggled underneath my bra, inching it up until it joined the other clothes on the floor, my panties following it after a minute. Now completely naked under him, I squirmed.

He looked amazingly clothed, but I didn't want to be the only one bare here.

Before he could reach for the paint, I tugged on a belt loop pointedly. "Off," I said, one word, but it held all my impatience.

Thomas didn't argue, instead reaching back to drag his shirt over his head, hands dropping to his pants, only for me to bat them away. I'd drooled over the thought of undressing him since we'd started dating, he didn't get to take that from me.

He froze at the first brush of my fingers, eyes smoldering as I carefully undid his belt and slid down the restricting fabric of his jeans. I couldn't completely drag them off from this angle, but he handled the rest. Kicking off everything but his underwear that now had a painful tent in it and a dark spot toward the top.

My mouth watered with the urge to taste it, but I forced the urge down. Not now, definitely later, though. Trailing the tips of my fingers against the defined outline, I bit back a moan at how big he was.

I'd felt him through his pants a few times now, but that was *nothing* compared to this.

He was thick, about the same as my wrist, and reached from the tip of my fingers to the base of my palm. A clench came from down south, arousal burning hot as I traced him through his underwear.

Before I could explore more, he gripped my hand and choked back a moan. "Woman, I adore you, but you need to stop doing that. I can only take so much, and we're already toeing the line."

Reluctantly I stopped, hand trailing to the free one of his resting above my head. "Fine, but I get to explore later."

His low chuckle vibrated through the otherwise quiet air. "Oh, trust me, you won't hear a single complaint from me. But for now..."

He shucked his underwear before coming to rest over me, his jutting length bobbing just over where I wanted him as he reached up for the paint.

It'd seemed like a good idea at the time, but now that he was there, looking like *that*, and so close to me, the last thing I wanted was to wait. It was too late now, though. I'd started this, and that meant I got to deal with the stifling arousal until he was done.

He picked the red paint, its bottle announcing that it was cherry flavored, before blotting a hefty amount on the center of my stomach. Using his fingers, he drew swirls outward from my belly button, not stopping until the entirety of my chest was covered.

Once he finished, it made a pretty picture, but I didn't have a chance to really appreciate it before he dropped down, warm and wet tongue sliding along the paths he'd made.

Sucking in a breath, I held it as he slowly made his way from one side of my stomach to the other before inching up closer to my breasts. Following the line of paint, he circled each one, curling tighter until his mouth latched onto my nipple and sucked.

Molten heat boiled in my groin, a weak moan pulling from me as I arched into him, repeating the motion when he moved onto the other nipple. When they were both puckered and red, he nodded in satisfaction before following the last trail he had left.

The one that went straight down.

Taking a bit more paint, he continued the line, making it swerve down until it rested just above my curls. Then he followed it, occasionally stopping to flick his tongue playfully against the skin he'd already cleaned.

When he hovered over the apex of my thighs, though, I shuddered. His breath hit in pants, the warm air heightening everything as I bucked up in a silent plea. One of his hands dropped to press the points of my hips back into the bed before he dug in with gusto.

Air shoved from my lungs in a heave when his curious tongue poked and prodded its way around, trailing over my outer lips before brushing the bundle of nerves at the top. I cried out, the broken sound pulling his attention as he focused on that nub.

Lips wrapped around it, sucking lightly as two fingers prodded lower, sliding in to the knuckle. I clenched around him, wanting more as he slowly pulled back before pressing in deeper. This time it was his turn to groan, the sound sending delicious vibrations through me.

"You're like a vice. Gonna feel *amazing* around me."

Stealing a glance down to where the red, almost purple head bobbed, I shuddered. Would he even fit? I'd never had more than my own fingers down there, and he was *far* bigger.

As if following my line of thought, he pressed a third finger in, a slight burn following it as he groaned, pulling on the bud again as he scissored his fingers.

The minor stretch faded after a minute, my eyes rolling back as he sank the digits all the way to the base of his palm and crooked them. He just barely scraped something, but whatever it was sent white across my vision.

Locking my thighs around his hand, I bucked to rub against it again with a cry. Distantly I heard his chuckle, felt it, but my brain was on melt down as he crooked his finger again, timing it with another pull that had my head spinning.

Just as I teetered on the edge, he pulled back.

The sudden loss made me hiss, eyes snapping open to meet his. "Thomas!" His name was more of a whine than anything, but he shook his head, eyes locked to his glistening fingers as he did.

"You're *soaked* and tighter than anything I could ever dream of. I want to feel you wrapped around me when you come." He growled,

127

hands a blur as he slid the condom on before shifting until the tip of his length pressed to my entrance.

Despite the almost feral lust, he paused, eyes meeting mine as he grit out, "Last chance. You good?"

Warmth bloomed in my chest, but I ignored it for now. In answer, I hooked my legs around his waist and dragged him closer. The tip pressed in, almost seeming like it wouldn't fit, before Thomas gripped my hips and lifted me slightly.

He popped in, the *fullness* of him against every one of my walls shoving the air from my lungs as I scrambled uselessly at the sheets. Taking his hand again to have something to hold on to, I forced myself to breathe through it as he gave tiny rocks of his hips.

Each one slid him just *that* much further in, the burn from before coming back with a vengeance as he slowly wiggled his way down. After who knows how long, he bottomed out, his balls brushing against me as my toes curled from the pressure.

"Virginia, talk to me." His words cut through the haze surrounding my mind, every syllable dripping with restraint as he held himself back from letting loose and giving us what we both wanted.

Throwing my arms around his neck, my nails dragging into his shoulders and raking down, I bucked hard against him and revealed the pulsing length twitching inside me. "I'm fine, now *go.*" The words were raspy, but they were all he needed.

Dragging back, he barely stayed out a second before sheathing himself again, the slick slide making a wet slapping noise as he picked up a steady pace. The band in my groin tightened in warning, every thrust inward nailing what had me seeing white earlier as little moans rained from me.

With a swivel of his hips and flick of his thumb against my entrance, I broke around him, hips snapping up to hilt him as he cursed above me. Hands dropped to my hips as he picked up speed, bottoming out on every slide until the pulsing between my legs grew more insistent.

Reaching down below us, I squeezed his balls and gave a final shudder when they tightened up in my hand. With one last *slap* of skin, he buried himself to the hilt and moaned.

Only his arm above his head kept him from crushing me, his hips canting in place as my clenching walls milked him for all he had. After a few minutes of shuddering aftershocks, he slid to a stop and pulled out, the flaccid length making my nose wrinkle before he collapsed next to me.

The only noise in the room was our breathing as we came back down to Earth, Thomas's arm winding around my waist as he all but melted into the sheets beside me. His skin was warm and sweaty pressed against mine, the size difference between us even more apparent as I folded into his arms like I'd always been there.

I fit against his chest perfectly, and something in me hummed in delight at that. As if we'd been made for each other.

Was it sappy and probably untrue? Yeah, but I also didn't care. After the hell with Steven, I'd earned the right to be sappy when I wanted.

Cuddling further into Thomas's chest, I sighed in bliss as we dissolved into a mass of limbs. One of his arms stretched out next to my head, and I inched over until my cheek rested on it. His free hand combed through my hair, the gentle pressure nearly sending me off to sleep before he spoke, the low rumble pulling my attention.

"Are you feeling all right?" he asked, and though I couldn't see his face, his tone had an undercurrent of concern.

Forcing my chin up so I could meet his eyes, I answered with a drowsy hum. "Never better, why?"

It was the truth; I'd never been this utterly and completely *happy*, not to mention relaxed. There'd always been something at the back of my mind, something to worry about, but now it was blissfully empty, my only focus being us.

I could get spoiled off this if he allowed.

His hand drifted down to stroke my hip, light tingles spreading out from the touch as he continued.

"Just a bit worried. Wasn't sure how the soreness would be afterward since I'm...bigger than you." The last few words were more of a mumble, but they succeeded in dragging one of my eyes up to his.

While he had the same sated expression I probably wore, beneath that, there was a disquiet I didn't like. This was really bugging him.

Good thing I knew how to fix it.

Pressing my palm flat to his chest, I guided him back until he sprawled underneath me. Once done, I shifted to lie on top of him, arms crossed with my propped up. Now I could comfortably look him in the eyes without neck strain *and* feeling his heartbeat underneath me was soothing.

Win-win.

Before I could get lost in that, I kissed his cheek and smoothed over the nerves still clear in his eyes. "Yeah, you are bigger than me, and *wow,* is that nice. Not just in the sexual way either." I paused to give him a teasing smile. "Though that's pretty freaking amazing too."

His lips twitched up, some of the dark edge to his eyes fading, and I took it as my go-ahead to continue.

Placing a hand on his jaw, I stroked the stubble and all but beamed. "Do you have any idea how nice it is to feel this? I can curl up into a ball, and you can *completely* wrap around me. I've never felt safe like this before, and it's awesome."

Like nothing in the world could touch me as long as I was here in his arms.

Understanding flashed behind his eyes before they softened and a wide smile inches across his lips. Well-muscled arms came up to wrap around me, pulling me tighter into him as the weight settled like a security blanket around me.

After a minute of soaking in the feeling like a cat, he nodded. "I like it too. How *is* the soreness, though? I doubt you escaped without any."

And the worry was back. I'd have to keep an eye on that. It was sweet of him to care that much, but I wasn't glass. I wouldn't break at the slightest jostle.

Though what we'd just done was probably more than a *slight* jostle.

Biting back the laugh bubbling up my chest at the thought, I responded. "Honestly, I don't feel anything yet. A mild burn if I shift the wrong way but even that isn't bad."

Finally, the tension in his frame eased, the worry completely disappearing as he rolled us over and wrapped himself around me. "Good, let me know if that gets worse. I'll draw a bath for you but until then…"

His mouth dropped to catch mine, my bottom lip sucked into his mouth in a heartbeat as he nipped it. A dulled rush of arousal pulsed hot in my veins, valiantly trying to gear up for a second round despite the languid warmth still rolling through me from the first one.

Tangling my arms up behind his head, I threw myself into the kiss, twining our tongues and sucking lightly, reveling in the light groan he gave.

Guess we'd be testing both our recovery periods today. I didn't have any complaints.

Chapter 12

I picked at my blouse for the fifth time in as many minutes, the urge to run back into my room and change overwhelming as Thomas sent a reassuring smile my way.

"It's fine. My parents already love you and the siblings you've met thus far do too. You have nothing to worry about," he soothed, a hand stroking down my back.

Logically I knew that, but the "meet the family" jitters weren't so easy to get rid of. And I'd be meeting the rest of his brothers today, not a small thing by any means.

Apparently, when they'd heard his mother had invited me over for dinner, they'd all decided it was time to come meet me. The thought was daunting.

Now we were headed out the door, and again, I swept a look down my frame. "Are you sure I shouldn't put on something nicer?" I liked this blouse, it was soft and comfy, but it wasn't exactly formal. It didn't have any holes in it or anything, but still.

Thomas snorted, pulling my attention away from my spiraling thoughts. "My family won't care. They'll just be happy you're there for them to tell embarrassing stories about me. Especially Adam, he knows most of them, and as my twin, he thinks it's his solemn duty to inform you of every stupid thing I've done since I was five."

That's right. I'd forgotten that he and Adam were twins. That'd be trippy until I got used to it. Accepting the arm he offered, I followed deftly, fighting back the wave of nerves still trying to drown me.

It's fine. Everything is going to go great. No need to freak out. It isn't as if his family is going to attack you.

They might lightly interrogate me, but that was it.

The thought wasn't as relieving as I'd hoped it would be.

The drive over was shorter than I'd preferred, and in no time, Thomas was pulling up outside a two-story house with a wraparound porch. Flowers lined the walkway up to the door, giving a splash of color to the brown brick home.

An air of *home* lingered around the place, and it only increased as Thomas led me up the drive. Wind chimes hung around, making soft music whenever the breeze hit.

A two-person swing sat near the door, alongside various hand prints pressed in cement leading up to the door. I paused when one of them caught my attention. It was Thomas's, though a much younger version of him.

Marveling at the tiny handprint, I crouched and experimentally held mine up to the cement. Talk about a growth spurt…

"I know, they all used to be that small, and some days it feels surreal to think they sprouted into the gentle giants they have today."

The voice made me whip around, hand clutched to my chest, and the only thing that stopped me from toppling backward was Thomas's quick grip on my arm.

Penelope stood behind us, Juan's arm wrapped around her waist, as she shot me an apologetic glance. "Sorry, I thought you'd hear me."

I took a deep breath to calm my still galloping heart and waved it off. "It's fine. I was just a bit distracted."

Penelope nodded in complete understanding before separating from her husband to pull Thomas into a hug. He returned it, arms just as careful as he was with me before she turned in my direction and—to my shock—repeated the motion.

Her shoulder was warm, and feeling her wrapped around me immediately reminded me of how safe I felt with Thomas. Without thought, I mumbled, "Your son gets his great hugs from you."

Distantly I heard Thomas snort, but Penelope absolutely *beamed* when she pulled back. "Darn right he did! Now come on, let's get you introduced to the brood. Everyone's been chomping at the bit to meet you."

And the nerves were back, great.

Before they could cause too much havoc, Thomas's arm settled at the base of my spine and he soothed. "Trust me; they're all happy to meet you. Drew hasn't stopped talking about you since we went on that hike with him, and Philip—his dad—has been meaning to meet you since. You already met Finn and Richard too. That just leaves Simon, Philip, and Adam. Vincent is working today, but he said it was fine since you've already met him."

It was still weird to hear just how many males were in his family. Props to his mother; I doubt I could have done it.

All thoughts of his mother and the hell the brothers probably caused growing up disappeared when we walked into the house.

Penelope waved us back into the living room, and there was the rest of the family.

Finn rested on the couch, an arm over the back as Drew cuddled into him. Richard sat at his side, occasionally retrieving the stuffed toy Drew dropped but otherwise happy to stay as an onlooker.

A man who looked exactly like Thomas stood near the wall, the similarities striking–duh, they're twins–and when he smiled, it was as if I were looking at Thomas himself. The only difference I could see was the slightly longer hair on Adam.

In my next heartbeat, he'd moved through the room to grab his twin in a hug, the soft cracks from his spine making me cringe internally.

"Hey! We were starting to think you'd never show up with your lady. No hiding her now, we all want to meet her."

Thomas rolled his eyes at his twin but returned the hug until another round of pops sounded.

When they separated, Adam turned to me with a cheeky grin. "And it's great to meet you formally! Thomas won't shut up about you on the days he helps at the dog rescue. Helena wanted to come today but her boy is down with the flu. Better to not risk spreading it."

He offered a hand, something I appreciated since I didn't want my spine cracked, and I took it. I'd barely had a chance to shake it before a different voice cut in.

"At least let her get comfy before you start on embarrassing Thomas."

Turning to the voice, I took in the man who was either Simon or Philip. Dirty blonde, almost brown hair was cut a few inches long, the lightest dusting of five o'clock shadow coating his jaw as he rolled his eyes.

He gently nudged Adam toward the couch before offering a hand. "Good to finally meet you. Drew hasn't stopped talking about the nice lady who went on the walk with him."

Heat slapped across my cheeks at the compliment as I took his hand. "Good to meet you too. Thomas mentioned that you were a doctor?"

Philip gave a so-so motion. "In training. I finished the college portion. Now it's on to the residency."

I didn't understand what that was, but honestly, I didn't think I had the extra mental space to ask right now. So I nodded with a smile, Drew himself coming over in a blur to latch onto Thomas's waist as if sensing we were talking about him.

"Hi, Uncle Thomas!"

The little voice rang in my ears, the volume taking me aback before I shook it off. Dully I heard Philip grumble about volume, but all my attention was on the kid as wide, imploring eyes swung to me.

"Hi! Can we go on another walk soon? The last one was fun."

I shot a glance at Thomas, leaving it up to him. I didn't mind if he didn't.

He must have caught that because he nodded. "Sure, but not today. Why don't you go help grandma in the kitchen?"

Drew beamed, disappearing in a blur of dark hair and flashing green eyes. Once he was gone, I chuckled. "Feels kind of like I got hit by a miniature hurricane of cuteness."

Philip snorted, "I get that a lot, though living with him has desensitized me to it for the most part."

I could imagine. Thomas led us both to the loveseat, the couch having just enough room for me to lean against his side. Once we were settled, the last of his brothers stepped forward for his introduction.

Dirty blonde hair leading into brown, just like Philip's, was a bit longer than his brothers. A neat beard sat on his chin, trimmed to almost regulation length, and a wide smile broke across his face as he offered his hand.

"Bout time he brought you over. After hearing about you from Richard, Finn, *and* Ma, I was starting to feel a bit left out. Name's Simon. Call me if you start any fires."

Wait…what?

Staring wide-eyed at him, I tried and failed to find words to say in response. Thankfully, Thomas stepped in with a roll of his eyes. "Simon is a firefighter."

Oh, that makes a lot more sense.

Confusion ebbed as quickly as it appeared, replaced by amusement over the mild joke. Apparently, I'd found the joker of the bunch, good to know. "I'll be sure to keep that in mind, though I'm usually pretty good about *not* setting things on fire. My name's Virginia."

Simon shrugged, moving back to take the spot next to Richard and Finn on the couch. Each of whom sent a wave my way but otherwise gave me space. Which I much appreciated. The room felt considerably smaller with the many towering males in here, and I was struggling to take it all in.

Before I could curl further into Thomas's side, he stood up, gesturing to Richard as he did. "Hey, I need to talk to you about something. Nothing bad, get that dam- dang look out of your eyes."

Richard eased, his shoulders having tensed when Thomas first spoke, and nodded. "All right, since the kitchen is taken, I take it we're going outside?"

Thomas nodded, only pausing to send a questioning look my way. Part of me wanted to go with them, I didn't know anyone else in the room, and it was mildly uncomfortable, but I had a hunch why Thomas was pulling Richard to the side.

Scarlet.

If he was talking to his brother about her, then I shouldn't be involved. It was too personal.

I nodded for him to go on, which he did after a long second of consideration. Once they were gone, I focused back on the others with a smile. "So, what about those embarrassing stories?"

Chapter 13

Thomas

"All right, now what's going on because I'm not buying that this is just a friendly chat. Does it have anything to do with the cops that were called to Virginia's work a few weeks ago?" Richard asked, sharp eyes digging in as I bit back the urge to curse.

It wasn't, but that was another thing I'd needed to talk to him about.

"Part of it. She's got a stalker that's on the loose after being in jail. I'll give you more details on that later. For now, it's about Scarlet," I said, bracing for the inevitable.

Sure enough, Richard tensed, every muscle from his toes up to his jaw tightening as he scowled.

"What about her? You know I don't like talking about this."

Yeah, he didn't, but my instincts were going fucking insane, and I needed *someone* to talk to. Considering it was at least partially him that was involved with this, it made sense to bring it to him.

That didn't mean it was going to make this topic any easier, though.

Choosing my words carefully, I started. "I know, but this is important, and it's driving me nuts. The last thing I needed was to *not* tell you and then have rumors hit you first. Would you prefer that?" Because if he did, then I'd bring it to Ma instead, but I doubted he'd go that route.

Sure enough, he shook his head.

"No, tell me. Though you already know I'm biased with anything to do with that woman," he said.

That woman, ouch.

Ice dripped from Richard's tone, and immediately I knew this was going to be a hard sell, but I had to do it. Something was off about the entire situation with him and Scarlet, and I wanted to know what was going on.

Even if it meant tearing open a wound Richard rarely ever poked.

"She defended Virginia from a slime in the market a bit ago. I managed to ask her some things and get *answers* for once." At that, Richard stood a bit straighter, a spark of offense clear.

He'd been trying to get answers from Scarlet for years; it'd definitely smart that I managed to do it within months of being home.

"Oh? More than she gave me," Richard said, venom oozing from his tone to cover the hurt that still lingered despite all the years that'd passed.

Yup, this wasn't going to be easy. Biting back a sigh, I continued. "Yeah, but that's not the point. I asked why she broke things off with you and she got flustered, *real* flustered. Helped that the slime brought your history up and rubbed it in her face. She was already off-kilter from that."

I might not have managed to get her to answer otherwise. Before Richard could speak up, probably with a cutting remark, I cut back in. "She kept saying she 'couldn't' talk about it. Not won't, can't. She said something changed before she broke things off, she wouldn't go into detail, but she mentioned her father. Then she mentioned she wanted to tell people about whatever it was, but it was too dangerous."

Now *that* caught Richard's attention. Eyes like that of a hawk sharpened, the old hurt shoved back under the weight of concern as his head snapped up.

"Dangerous? For her?"

Something lethal lingered under his tone, and I shrugged, hating that I didn't have more information. "I don't know, maybe. When I tried to ask more, she freaked, saying she couldn't say anything else. Before she left, she told me that 'no,' she didn't break things off with you because she wanted to. And everything she's saying to this point smacks of foul play."

The more I thought about it, the uglier the picture got. It was well known that her old man hated our entire family. After his wife died, he turned to the bottle, drowning himself in alcohol. He lost his martial arts studio to debts over his own addiction, not us, but like most alcoholics, he refused to accept the blame for his own actions.

Which led to him blaming us.

Locking eyes with Richard, I finished. "Her father has hated us from the start, even more so after he lost his studio. Now we're learning that Scarlet *had* to break things off with you because it was too 'dangerous' because everything changed? This isn't painting a pretty picture, Richard."

His lips thinned into a hard line, but he nodded to show he agreed. "No, it isn't. But right now, we're only going off of a hunch and a few sentences from her that may or may not be truthful."

Irritation flared hot in my chest, but before I could bitch him out, he cut me off with a glare. "Look, Thomas. The entire first year after our break-up, I *tried* to get her to talk to me. I tried and she refused. She could have come to me at any point, and I would have listened. She knew me better than anyone back then. For her not to do that? It's a blaring sign she doesn't want my help."

His mouth pinched at the corners, old pain coming to the surface again as he shook his head. "I'll try to talk to her *one* more time, if for no other reason than to get the truth from her lips, but after that, this is finished. And I don't expect anything to come from this either. She's refused to talk to me this long. She won't stop now."

With that, he turned to walk back inside, but before I could move to follow, he pulled up short. He gave a low sigh of exhaustion before saying over his shoulder. "Thanks for telling me this. You're right that I wouldn't have wanted to hear it through the rumor mill. Just…I'm tired of trying for this woman, Thomas. I tried for a *year* before, constantly dealing with the rejection and the what-ifs. It nearly tore me apart then, and I swore to never do this to myself again."

Guilt tugged on my gut before I shoved it down. I already knew when I brought this to him it wasn't a good subject, but that damn instinct of mine screamed that there was more at play than what we were seeing.

And if that was the case, maybe Richard could work things out with Scarlet because, say what he will, I knew that look in his eyes. He might be hurt, but he still carried that torch for Scarlet, and if the look in *her* eyes that day in the market was any indication?

She did too.

But it was up to them. I gave him the information, and now the ball was in his court. Moving forward to clasp his shoulder, I offered.

"I get that, and if I wasn't at least decently sure there was more going on here, then I wouldn't have brought it up to you. I'm not doing this because I like seeing you shredded, but my neck is on *fire* with the feeling that something isn't right."

Richard nodded, patting my shoulder before heading back inside.

Pausing long enough to take a centering breath, I followed. That conversation had gone better than I'd expected to be honest. Now, with any luck, Scarlet would tell him everything and we could start getting to the bottom of this mess.

Chapter 14

Virginia

Thankfully, when Thomas and Richard came back, neither of them looked the slightest bit ruffled. No fist fight then; that was good.

Richard looked a bit paler than normal, though not surprising given the topic.

He caught my eyes, probably noticing my worry, and gave me a tired smile. All things considered, I'm impressed it was genuine.

Thomas came back to his previous seat, arm settling around my shoulders as he dipped low and whispered just loud enough for me to hear. "He's fine. Said he'll check it out. Now it's up to Scarlet to tell him everything. If she doesn't, then there's nothing we can do about it."

For her sake, I hope she just told Richard everything. Whatever she was hiding smacked of trauma, and the more I learned, the less I liked it.

But Thomas was right; we couldn't do anything about it now. Better to focus on the present and work our way through it.

Thankfully, the rest of the dinner went fine, Drew taking turns with Simon and Finn peppering me with questions. Occasionally,

Philip, Richard, or Thomas would back them off, but for the most part, the conversation was easy.

By the time we finished eating, I had a better idea of who each brother was—an achievement in and of itself—and there was a pleasant buzz in the air. Belonging settled in my bones, the feeling of being *home* making a balloon of happiness swell in my chest.

This was what it was like to be in a family.

I'd given up hope of ever feeling it for myself.

Once the dishes were done—something I insisted on helping with since I didn't do anything else—Thomas and I were preparing to get going, only to pause when Richard breezed over. The tension to his shoulders was gone now, though something sharp still lingered in his eyes.

It didn't show in his smile, though, or his tone when he spoke. "Looks like you'll fit in just fine with the family, unsurprisingly. And about Scarlet…"

I straightened, tensing on habit as he chose his words carefully.

"I'll look into it, but don't hold your breath. She told you guys more in one day than she has me in years," he said, tone prickly with pain, and without a thought, I soothed it.

"If it helps any, I don't think it has much to do with *who* was asking her. Before Thomas came, some guy was harassing me, and she tried to send him packing. He brought you up, though, and she just… crumbled. That's when Thomas showed up and started asking her

148

things. If it weren't for what that guy said, I don't think she would have."

She'd already been taken off guard, so she'd answered honestly when Thomas asked her those things.

Some of the pain left Richard's eyes as he sighed. "Maybe, but if that's the case she probably won't tell me anything later. I'll still try, just...don't expect much. She's damn good at keeping secrets when she wants to."

I nodded, patting his arm with a smile. "You can only do your best. Asking anything over that from someone isn't right. And who knows? Maybe she'll surprise you."

He gave me a disbelieving hum but let the subject drop. Turning back to Thomas, he dragged the taller man into a bone-crushing hug, which was quickly returned before he ambled back into the house.

Once we were alone again, Thomas raked a hand through his hair–as much as he could with how short it was–before gesturing to the kitchen.

"I gotta say bye to Ma before we leave. She'll hold it against me for the next five years otherwise," he said, amusement clear even through the exasperation.

I didn't doubt it. Penelope was the sort to tease relentlessly, and this was no different. Linking my arm with his, I nudged us forward.

"I'll go with you. I wouldn't want her to think I'm avoiding her or anything."

Thomas nodded before leading us to the other room. Penelope sat at the kitchen table, Juan at her side, as they chatted. When we entered, though, both heads turned our way, and Penelope instantly moved to stand.

Swinging her arms wide open, she accepted her hug from Thomas with ease. "It was good to see you again. While I understand why you went into the military, having you home is relieving. Your spot was awfully empty until now," she said, barely loud enough to be audible.

Thomas's grip tightened just a bit before she pulled back, patting his cheek. "But you're back now, and that's all that matters."

Then she turned to me, smile wide as she dragged me into a hug next. This time I was ready for it, sinking into the warm embrace with relish as I soaked in the feelings. I'd never had a motherly figure before, and Penelope was seamlessly sliding into that spot as if it'd been made for her.

Maybe it was. Who knew?

Separating after a minute, I smiled as Penelope waved a playful finger at me. "And *you* had better not be a stranger. We have dinner at the same time every day. All the kids have a standing invitation, and that's the same for you. Come whenever you can."

My heart squeezed, but I didn't show it outwardly. Instead, I nodded, biting back a chuckle when she added on after a minute, looking at Thomas sternly.

"You better bring her back here soon, you hear?"

Thomas nodded, his smile not slipping as Penelope hummed in satisfaction, Juan stepping forward to pat his son's shoulder.

"Give me a call whenever you have a day free. It'll be nice to go out shooting like we used to," he said, tone steady. Then his eyes trailed to me, and he added on, "And of course you're invited as well. If you want to be there, chica."

I nodded without hesitation, not even bothering to consider it. Thomas's entire family was nice, and having a day out with his father wouldn't be a hardship.

Moving out of the kitchen, we were stopped on our way to the door by Philip, Drew cuddled contently in his arms, mouth open and drooling on his shoulder. It made a cute sight, I had to admit.

Before I could ask the tired but happy-looking father if he wanted me to get a picture for him—the moment was just *too* cute— Philip spoke with an exhausted smile.

"It was good meeting you, Virginia. I hope to see you more often at family dinners. Though my schedule makes attendance sporadic at best." He ended the statement on a grimace, and Thomas cut in with a snort.

"You're a *dad*, Philip. We're not gonna complain about you not showing up. You got your residency, Drew, and us to balance. We know that sometimes family will have to wait," Thomas said, understanding clear as he patted Drew's back. The boy squirmed a bit, cracking a tired eye open to smile at his uncle before dozing back off.

Philip snorted at that, shaking his head lightly. "Well, I need to get this one home. He's getting too big for me to carry comfortably…"

He moved for the door, but not before I heard Drew's quiet grumble. "I don't wanna be too big." Philip gave him a resigned smile.

"Unfortunately, it's not up to either of us; now, get some sleep. We can talk about it more later." The end faded as they moved further away, Thomas and I going in the opposite direction once we got outside.

Once we were comfortably settled in the car and headed back, Thomas spoke, the noise jarring in the otherwise silent vehicle. "I told you they'd love you."

Yeah and I'd never been happier for him to be right.

"You did, and a part of me believed you, but it's hard to think that after so many years of not having a family, yours accepted me so easily." Darker memories edged forward as I sighed. "I'd been through dozens of families when I was a kid, and something always made them drop me back off. Too quiet, too loud, not polite enough, the reason always changed."

I looked out the window, ignoring the pang that hadn't faded no matter how many years passed. "After getting rejected so many times it's a novel concept to think acceptance is real."

But it was and today I'd felt it in full. I wish I could go back and tell the younger me to just hold on, it got better. I wouldn't have believed it, but still.

The car pulled up out front of my house, Thomas moving to get my door before I had a chance to reach for the handle. Only instead of following me inside, Thomas gripped my elbow and stopped us outside the door.

His eyes stared down at me like a puzzle he couldn't quite figure out but was determined to manage. One of his hands trailed up to cup my cheek, thumb stroking lightly as he spoke.

"It's real, and anyone who let you go was an idiot. But that works in my family's favor since that means we get to adopt you. Trust me, Ma is already mentally filling out the papers as we speak. You have a family now, even if we are a little insane at times."

My heart swelled uncomfortably, pushing against my chest like a balloon with too little room as I nodded. Words failed me, but I knew a way I could get what I was feeling across without them.

Trailing a hand up into his hair, I tugged him down into a kiss. Heady warmth started in my stomach before branching outward, inching through my veins until there wasn't an inch of me left untouched.

I had somewhere to belong now, and it was with him and his family. Definitely not something I'd seen coming, but I'd never take it for granted either.

Arms wrapped around me, dragging me against his frame until not a centimeter of space remained. His heart beat slammed against mine, the thud of it loud against my ear as I settled onto his chest. Silence drifted between us, neither of us in a hurry to break it.

Words weren't necessary, not right now.

All that mattered was how we felt and when we pulled back, I glanced up to catch the adoring gaze locked on me. Without a doubt, I knew what I wanted.

Twining our fingers, I tugged him inside, past the dozing Bello and toward my room. Once the door shut behind us, I led him to the bed and pressed a palm to his chest.

He followed the silence directive, eyes sharp on me as I retrieved what was left of the edible paint. I'd never gotten my turn with him before, and I'd say it was more than time to rectify that.

The sight of the bottle lit his eyes up with excitement, and immediately his fingers drifted to his shirt hem. Before he could disrobe, I caught his hand and shook my head.

"Let me do it," I said, voice quiet but certain. He didn't argue, scooting back until he lay in the middle of the bed, arms behind his head. The pose was tantalizing, but I couldn't let myself get distracted yet.

Sitting by his side, I gripped the hem of his shirt and slid it slowly up his frame, setting it to the side once he was free of it. My fingers hooked in the waistband of his jeans, stroking the soft hair leading down to his groin as he sucked in a breath and held it.

The muscles in his arms bunched, but he didn't move, letting me go at my own pace as I carefully undid his jeans and slid them down too. Once he was completely free of clothes, I reached for the paint, only to pause when he cleared his throat.

"I believe you're forgetting something," he said, eyes flicking down my still clothed frame. I hadn't actually, but considering I'd demanded him to strip last time, I'd say it was fair play for it to be reversed.

That didn't mean I couldn't tease him a bit, though.

Making sure to sit so he could get the best possible angle, I curled my fingers and *slowly*–even more so than I'd done with his– stripped my shirt. Every movement was played up, tension crackling through the air like lightning by the time I'd slid off my underwear.

His eyes stayed glued to me, pupils blown wide as his length stirred, rising to the occasion. I gave it a long look, my mouth water at the sight, I forced myself not to give in. At least not yet. I had plans for now, and they didn't involve that *just* yet.

Reaching for the paint, this time without being stopped, I dropped a small dot in the center of his chest. Then the fun began. He'd done basic swirls on me, more focused on getting to the main event to do anything detailed, but it was my turn now, and I *had* the patience.

At least, I'd make myself have it.

I started slowly, the same swirls he'd used moving between his pectorals before branching out. Once I got to his nipples, though, I changed tactics. He'd done spirals around mine, but I wanted something different.

Using the center as the base, I made tiny flower petals around them, a yellow–banana flavored, not my favorite, but it'd do–sunflower

155

sat on each side of his chest. It wasn't detailed by any means, but I could tell what it was.

With that done, I switched colors of paint to red and dropped a bit in my palm. Using the fingers of my other hand, I started directly over the center of his chest and made a heart. Was it anatomically placed correctly? No.

Did I care? Also no.

And if the gooey softening to his eyes was any indication, he didn't either.

Branching off from the first heart, I made vine-like waves moving across his chest, occasionally stopping to sprout more hearts. Once the small amount of red paint was gone, I nodded in satisfaction before reaching for the green one next.

If I was going to make my all too willing boyfriend into a painting, I may as well do it right and go all out. Turning to get a better angle, I pressed my finger to where the red stopped–just over his navel–and started downward.

Branching out like roots, I slowly thinned the veins until they all intersected at his groin. Getting the paint out of hair was a pain, but one we'd both thoroughly embraced. Still, I tried my best to keep most of it on his skin and just over his pubes.

His length stood to attention now, the tip leaking and flushed an angry red. Swiping a thumb over the slit, I bit back a smile when Thomas hissed, his hips bucking sharply before he pressed them down with a groan.

Good, I was enjoying this too much for him to take over yet.

Starting at the base of him, I traced the thick vein on his underside with paint before making a spiral from tip to bottom. I almost put flowers there, too, before a glance up changed my mind. His jaw was clenched tight, restraint barely holding.

He was being nice, letting me go as long as I had, and I didn't want to repay that by teasing him longer than was necessary.

Besides, I could do that next time.

Sucking one of my fingers into my mouth to clean off the last of the paint, I paused when Thomas groaned, eyes sliding shut as his head dropped against the blankets.

"That's fucking *hot*," he growled, the vibrations from it traveling through his chest and up the thigh I had pressed against him. They traveled south, sitting between my thighs with relish as I swallowed.

I hadn't actually meant for that to be a tease–I really liked the mint flavor of the green paint–but now that he said something...

Locking eyes with him, I grabbed the paint and squeezed some onto my hand, letting it trail from my wrist down my fingers. His eyes followed every bit of it, locked on as if he'd die if he looked away. Raising my hand to my mouth, I slid a long lick from the wrist up, up, up.

His eyes fluttered shut, mouth twisting as his length twitched, another bead of clear liquid sliding down as he shuddered. "Woman, I'm trying to behave, but you're not making it easy. If you're not going to let me fuck you, *at least* give me your hand."

At first, I didn't realize what he meant, but when his tongue flicked out to wet his lips, understanding dawned.

I had actually been about to move things along, but that was too intriguing to pass up.

Letting my hand hover over his jaw, I nodded, watching as he opened his mouth and slid his tongue along the path the paint left. The rough surface swept waves of tingles through me, adding to the growing pulse between my thighs as he rumbled.

"Mint. Never thought I'd like it but anything tastes good on you."

I hadn't known he didn't like mint. Keeping that in mind for future reference, I sucked in a breath when he sucked two of my fingers into his mouth and *pulled*. The bundle at my entrance tingled, memories of him doing that further down shivering to the surface as his tongue flicked out to collect every last bit of paint.

Once there was no more, he let the finger slide out, shiny with spit. An obscene-sounding *pop* came as he released the last of them, repeating the action until my hand was clean.

He was right; that *was* hot.

Warmth crawled through my collar, nearly making me woozy with it as I lowered my hand back to his chest, careful to avoid the patterns there.

I wasn't going to last much longer if he kept looking at me like that, so it was better I got a move on.

Lowering myself down to be level with his chest, I started at the sunflowers. Each petal was meticulously cleaned, his muscles tensing under me as he stopped to suck and roll each nipple as he'd done to me before.

His chest vibrated with a groan even as I moved on to the hearts sprawling his chest. Taking my time, I slowly trailed from the top of his collarbone down to where the red paint ended at his navel. By the time I hovered over the jutting length, his teeth were sunk into his lip, and he'd squeezed his eyes shut.

Every breath was strained as if forced out of his lungs, and that was when I took pity on him.

Kissing the tip, the salt of him battling with the sweeter taste of the paint, I started the last of my trek. The spiral was first, skin and muscle jumping under my mouth as he fought to not buck up and choke me.

Once his hair tickled my nose, I shifted to the last bit of paint. The stripe covering the throbbing vein leading up. It pulsed in time with his heartbeat, an answering clench moving through my groin when he gave tiny twitches up.

I gave one last, long lick to clear the rest before sitting back, marveling at the sight in front of me.

Thomas was gorgeous, laid out, skin flushed fluorescent as he heaved in air like he'd run a marathon. His length jerked as if looking for more friction, and when he opened his eyes again, they were hazy with lust.

"Put me out of my misery," he groaned, and almost pleaded to his tone as he bucked his hips again. Shooting a glance down to his balls that were dangerously close to his frame–a warning I knew all too well–I did just that.

During my little exploration, arousal slicked my folds, nearly sliding down to coat my thighs as I swung a leg up and over his waist.

Pausing long enough to snag a condom from the nightstand, I slid it from tip to base, reveling in the shudder he gave at the feather-light contact.

I could ride him from here, but after today, after soaking in the feeling of finally *belonging* somewhere, I didn't want that. No, I wanted to belong to someone, to him.

I'd ride him a different day. He already showed he didn't mind handing over the reins in this aspect, and right now, I wanted to be claimed.

Tugging on his arms, I guided us back until it was him hovering over me. A flash of confusion sparked, before I spoke, clearing it instantly.

"I got my fill for now. Your turn." Lacing my arms up above his head, my thighs opening in invitation, I purred. "And Thomas? Don't stop, and *don't* hold back. I want to think about you buried balls deep anytime I sit down tomorrow."

I generally tried to avoid dirty talk–the words never seeming to come out right from me–but his reaction was instantaneous.

His frame locked above me, breath skidding to a stop as his throat bobbed hard and his restraint snapped.

A firm grip hauled me off the bed, spinning me to face the headboard and wall as his firm chest pressed against my back. His palm spread across the center of my back, pushing me to lean forward as his other hand tugged my knees further apart.

The head brushed my entrance, my spine bowing to give it a better angle as Thomas's hands settled on my hips, stroking and firm just as he nestled the tip between my lips and waited.

Anticipation climbed as his mouth brushed my throat, teeth scraping lightly as he spoke in a tone dripping with command. "Hold on tight, and don't you dare hold back your screams."

That was the only warning he gave. His hips snapped forward as his hands jolted me back, the resounding *clap* of skin ringing in my ears as he hilted himself in one slide.

Air shoved from my lungs, the fullness just as intense as the first time, only now he didn't pause. Leaning most of his weight over me, he yanked back only to drill back in, his length rubbing deliciously against every spot I had.

My walls clenched around him, slick arousal easing what would have been a painful pace otherwise as he adjusted his grip and fucked me in earnest.

Leaning forward on the headboard, I let my head fall against the wall with a thump as he thrust to the base, dragging himself back only to repeat the motion not a second later. I clamped around him, molding to his shape as he ruthlessly chased his release.

Wet slaps echoed through the room, my cut-off gasps and his groans making for a naughty symphony as he rutted hard enough to send my hips into the headboard with a *crack!*

He paused, but before he could ask if I was all right–the man was too sweet for his own good sometimes–I clenched around him like a vice and threw myself back on his length.

His hiss brushed my ear, and he took the wordless reassurance for what it was. An arm wound around my waist, lifting me up just a bit until my knees didn't brush the bed, my only contact coming from him as he plunged up into me.

An arm braced over my head, keeping us in place as he started pulsing inside me. Every thrust forward sent his balls smacking into my entrance, grazing a spot I couldn't reach from our current position as his rhythm faltered, ruts becoming frantic as he groaned.

"Tell me you're close."

I nodded, my answer breaking on a cry. "Yes, yes. Just a little —"

He shifted his hand, arm not moving from around my waist as he did until his thumb rolled the knot of nerves at my entrance. Risking a glance down, my eyes rolled back. I was stretched obscenely around him, my arousal making his condom wrapped length shiny as bits of it hit the sheets underneath us.

Watching as he buried himself to the hilt, his fingers doing a clever twist at the same time, I shattered around him. Throwing my head back, a gasp that might have been his name ripped from me as I bucked against him, writhing through the aftershocks as the tightness released and my vision went white.

His curse hit my ear through the dull buzzing stuffing my head, his pace picking up again with none of his previous grace until he was rutting up like an animal only after one thing.

Shunting himself to the base, I came back to myself just in time to feel him break. His hips slowed, languid rolls forward stopping after a minute as he sucked in air like a dying man.

The arm around my waist lowered me, muscles shaking as we both recovered from the intense experience.

His length slid out, a small trail of liquid going with him as I shuddered. Empty, I'd never thought the feeling would bother me before, but after having him stretch me full I definitely *didn't* like it.

But I could fix that later. For now, we both needed to recuperate.

Thomas inched back before dragging both of us to lie on the blankets, arms tangled into each other as my head thumped soundlessly onto his chest. A dull soreness tugged from below, but I'd never been more satisfied.

He'd done exactly what I'd asked for, and if he was willing, I'd be hitting him up for this more often, no doubt.

Snuggling closer when a chill swept through the air, the sweat making everything feel colder as I calmed down, I sighed when his arms wrapped securely around me again.

When my brain wasn't circling Venus anymore, I tilted my head back and rested it on his outstretched arm. From this angle, I got a clear view of Thomas and what a sight he made.

His mouth was slightly parted, still recovering from the earth-shattering orgasm he'd had, and his eyes were half-lidded. When he noticed I was watching him, alertness edged away the haze until he focused on me with considerably less of his usual sharpness.

"You good, baby?" he asked, voice low and stroking along my spine like a caress. The nickname was also new, and I'd definitely be badgering him to use it more often. Ignoring the pleasant shivers that two syllables brought, I nodded.

"More than good; I'm great. What are the odds I can convince you to do that often? Like, at least once a month, maybe more?" The words were hardly a hum, my exhaustion slurring everything together, but Thomas understood.

His lips twitched up tiredly as he chuckled. "As often as you like, I'm definitely down for that." Sucking in a deep breath, he smiled. "Damn, I thought what we did before was nice. This blew it completely out of the water."

Agreed.

"And it'll only get better the more we explore," I said, mind drifting to all the things we still hadn't done. Apparently, from behind was definitely an amazing position and it was definitely on our to -be-repeated list.

Maybe I'd get one of those position books people were always raving about. If the payoff was more times like this, it was *more* than worth it.

Thomas nodded, breaking me from my thoughts as he tied off the condom and threw it into the garbage next to the bed. Once done, he tucked me into him again, mouth brushing my head before sighing. "Something tells me I should be working on my flexibility…"

At that, a grin curled my lips, some of my energy coming back as I teased. "Oh, definitely. And I'll be right there with you."

His groan was more playful than real, the smile still twitching across his lips proving that. "Something tells me stretching with you will make a whole lot less exercise get done."

He paused, considering that before revising. "Well, it'll be a different kind of exercise."

Biting back a laugh, I shrugged innocently. "Probably, but I, for one, would regret nothing."

Which was true. The idea of getting to see *him* in stretchy yoga pants was enough for regular stretches to sound like a fantastic idea.

Not that his usual jeans were anything to sniff at either.

Shaking the thought to the side, my eyes trailed to the clock on the wall. It was getting late, and unfortunately, that meant Thomas would have to go soon. As if seeing the same thing, he groaned.

"I don't want to go, but I didn't leave enough food for Naomi and she still has to be let out for the night."

Naomi wasn't with him, and it wasn't fair to leave her alone overnight without extra food. But there was an easy solution to that.

Rolling over to lean on his side, I offered, "You could bring her here for the night? I know we haven't actually done the whole 'spend the night' thing, but if you'd be interested...?"

I let it trail off, but before nerves could strike, Thomas nodded. The frown tugging his lips smoothed out into a smile as he dropped a kiss against my head.

"Sounds like a plan to me. I shouldn't be long. Need me to pick anything up on the way back?" he asked, getting out of bed with obvious reluctance.

After a beat of thought, I shook my head. "Nope, just bring you and your adorable dog. That's all I need. I'm sure Bello will appreciate the company too."

Thomas shot me a look, eyes warm and soft at the edges before he visibly pulled himself back. "Right, gotta get used to you saying stuff like that. I'll be back. I need to get out of here before I leave poor Naomi."

With that, he scooped up his shirt, jeans already—tragically—in place as he loped for the door. Smart of him. If he'd stayed much longer, I'd probably pull him into another round.

Distantly, I registered the sound of the door shutting before I flopped back on the bed, a wide and probably goofy smile curling my lips.

This was what I'd avoided all these years. On the one hand, I was glad I didn't get with anyone else. On the other, it wasn't half as terrifying as I'd thought it would be.

Thomas was a sweetheart to the bone, despite his towering form leading others to believe differently, and I doubted I could ever be happier with anyone else.

Forcing sore muscles up from the bed, I snagged my robe and stood. The mention of feeding Naomi reminded me I still had to get Bello's food down. I'd given him some that morning, but he was picky about his feeding times.

No reason to invite potential interruptions into later.

I could just see it now, Thomas and I wrapped into another round of love-making, and somehow, someway, Bello manages to get in to demand his food.

He'd done it before, found impossible ways to get to me all because he was hungry, and he demanded sustenance *right that minute*.

I loved that brat, but sometimes he was too much.

Finding my furry companion took hardly any time at all. He lounged contently on his cat tower like usual, but when he noticed what direction I was walking in, he darted to start wrapping around my ankles.

Chuckling at the display, I mumbled, "Yeah, you know exactly where I'm going. Food time."

He only stopped when I pulled the can down and dropped it in his bowl, too busy burying his face in the food to care.

Stepping back with a shake of my head, I moved to the bedroom again, only to freeze as every hair on my body stood to attention.

Eyes drilled against the back of my head, my stomach dropping to my shoes as ice slid through my veins.

Damn it, not tonight. Things were going well and I didn't want my paranoia to ruin it now!

Despite the logical part of my mind that said not to check, I couldn't help it. The compulsion pulled at me until I found myself by the window, scanning the yard.

Nothing, just like I figured.

Releasing a long sigh of relief, I forced my shoulders to loosen from their tense line. *Steven being out is frying my nerves, and the sooner he is caught, the better.*

Turning back to pet Bello, I froze.

Bello had left his food half-eaten, his face now turned toward the living room and his fur puffed out aggressively. Hissing flowed from him unlike any I'd heard before, and the sound sent a sliver of unease up my spine.

"Bello?" I asked, looking in the direction he was, only for everything to come crashing down when I noticed it.

A silhouette, bathed completely in darkness thanks to my curtains being drawn.

A silhouette that was looking at me as he stepped forward into the light.

Steven.

Chapter 15

He towered over me, light from the nearby window painting him in an eerie glow as he stepped forward.

Every muscle in my body tensed, adrenaline crashing through me as the urge to run screamed in my veins. But I couldn't. Like a deer in headlights, I was stuck.

Tremors wracked my legs, nearly sending me to the floor as all the strength I had evaporated, running with its tail between its legs at the sight of *him*.

And when he spoke, it was all I could do not to lose my lunch.

His smile was average, nothing out of the ordinary, but the insane glint in his eyes slid ice down my spine as he casually took another step forward. "It took longer than I thought to get a minute alone with you. That lummox was always at your hip. Rude of him, keeping me from your side, but more importantly…"

He trailed off, insanity growing until wide eyes watched me with sick glee and affront, the orbs all but bulging out. "How rude of *you*, cheating on me with someone else. And after all I've done for you. I left you dozens of gifts before and you repaid me by throwing me in that hellhole. Now I'm out, trying to communicate with you, and you choose *him*?"

The smile finally dropped, but the scowl that took its place wasn't any better. Sharp as glass and something lethal lingering just under the surface.

My skin crawled just looking at him.

When he took another step forward, I finally snapped out of my stupor. Looking around for anything that could be used as a weapon, I replied while carefully stepping back.

"I already told you, I have no interest in anything being between us. I never have and I never will. Therefore I wasn't 'cheating' because we were never together. Who I date is entirely my own decision," I said, coming up empty on weapons in the living room.

The kitchen would at least have knives if I could just get there without him getting a hold of me.

Bello stayed puffed up at my feet, hissing madly as Steven spared a glance down at it. He snorted. "The stupid hell-cat is still the same, I see."

Then, before I could move to intervene, he reeled back and slammed a boot into Bello's side. A choked cry wrenched from my lungs, but before I could do more than lean forward, Bello lunged into action.

With a yowl that made every hair on my neck stand to attention, he jumped on Steven with all claws bared. Latching onto Steven's chest, he refused to let go as the man visibly lost his arrogance and started spitting curses.

"Stupid fucking cat, should have damn well killed you when I had the chance!" He tried to swing at Bello, but missed, my furry savior dodging before jumping in for another round.

Shaking off my surprise at the entire spectacle, I spun on my heel and ran for the kitchen knives. Standing here and gawking sure wasn't helpful, and I'd be damned before I let him hurt my cat.

Just as I managed to grip the meat cleaver, its blade heavier than the rest but also sharper, Steven staggered into the kitchen, Bello not in sight.

A spark of terror lanced up my spine at his absence before I shoved it down. I could check on him in a minute. I needed to take care of Steven. Leveling the knife in front of me, I tried to put on a brave face despite the shake threatening to make me drop the knife.

"Stay back! I don't want to use this knife, but I *will*."

I would, though I'd probably puke once the adrenaline wore off. Steven shot an amused glance down at it but stopped just out of range. Blood trailed down his face in rivers, Bello's work no doubt, painting an even more deranged picture.

"You can't do shit; don't try to paint yourself as some kind of fighter. I know better. I've followed you for months. You haven't taken any training. You're just as weak as you always were," he taunted, mouth pulled into a nasty sneer as I fought the urge to wince at the truth there.

I'd meant to take a class in self-defense since the day he'd been put away, but there's always been something to do. I regret that now.

But that didn't mean I was just going to lower the knife and play the damsel in distress. Thomas would be back soon; I just had to hold Steven off that long. I may not have any formal training, but I *did* have a larger-than-life knife.

It would have to be enough.

Squaring my shoulders, I forced a certainty I didn't feel into my voice. "Doesn't matter. Even without training, this knife could still do damage, and that's all that matters."

Steven's arrogance flagged, eyes flicking down to the glinting blade with open wariness before his mask slid back into place. "Not if I take it from you."

He lurched as if to do just that, adrenaline hitting like a punch as I instinctively slashed the knife and shuddered when it made contact. Blood coated the blade as Steven's pained howl split the air, a diagonal cut across his nose almost into his eye adding to the injuries Bello had given him.

He staggered back, hands rising in an attempt to slow the blood flow as his face twisted into a snarl. "You bitch!"

This time he kept his distance, but it wasn't a comfort. The insanity from before had sharpened into something murderous. Before, he'd been looking at me with lust, his intent obvious, but now?

No doubt, if he got his hands on me, he'd be ending it.

Tightening my grip around the knife handle, the sweat beading at my palms not making it easy, I puffed up. "Get out of here! Thomas will be back any minute, and while I'm *not* trained, he is."

And right now, the thought of the safety he brought was enough to make me want to weep. I could use that and his strength.

Steven flicked a glance outside as if to check for himself that Thomas wasn't there before he scoffed. "Are you forgetting that I've been watching you? He never stays the night, not like I do. Did you feel me nearby? I stayed. Every. Single. Night."

The words dripped with deranged lust and I fought against the souring in my stomach. I'd thought I was just being paranoid lately…

Apparently not.

Steven must have noticed my unease because he purred, smile coming back. "Ah, you did notice. And you even pushed that stupid shelf in front of my favorite peephole. It made watching you a lot more boring this time around. I didn't even get good material to fuck myself to."

Outrage twinged just under the surface as if it were somehow *my* fault that he didn't get to play out his twisted fantasies.

The human mind was a weird and terrifying thing.

Putting aside the offense at his complete arrogance over what he believed owed to him, I shrugged airily. Maybe if I could keep him talking, then it would give Thomas time to show up. The drive to his place wasn't far, and he'd already been gone…

Actually, how long *had* he been gone? Time was weird, and right now, every second felt like a year. Maybe he was right around the corner or maybe he was only just getting home.

There was no way of knowing until he pulled into the driveway. Better to stall until he came.

"Too bad for you. Why don't you go find someone to hump if it means that much to you. Someone that *isn't* me," I said, already knowing he wouldn't drop his fixation, but at this point, it didn't hurt to try.

Sure enough, he scoffed. "Well, there's the problem, I don't *want* anyone else. From the day I walked into your therapy session, I knew you were it for me. No one else will do, and I will have you."

Before I had a chance to tell him just how much that wasn't happening, he jumped forward. His hand grabbed the blade of the cleaver, the knife sinking in as he jerked back and sent it flying. More blood gushed from his palm, but a satisfied smile curled his lips.

"There, now what will you do? You don't have a weapon." He took a step forward, caging me back into the counter as he reached for me.

Only for a low hiss to split the air a second before Bello lunged onto Steven's back. Relief hit like a tidal wave as he staggered away from me, Bello firmly latched on and not out of his reach as he desperately tried to get the feline off.

Thank God he hadn't hurt Bello too badly. From what little I could see, he wasn't injured, so maybe Steven had stunned him or something. It didn't matter. Bello was tearing at my assailant with all the rage of a tiger.

He was getting fresh fish for the next week, at least.

Before I could go for another weapon, my head spinning from adrenaline, the sound of tires on gravel came, and relief hit again, nearly knocking my knees out from under me.

Without thought, I called loud enough to hopefully be heard outside. "Thomas, he's here!"

I didn't get anything else out, Steven finally managing to dislodge Bello long enough to swing on me. His fist cracked across my jaw, pain exploding as tears burned my eyes. Even through that, though, I heard the sound of pounding footsteps making their way toward us in the house.

Apparently, Steven caught it too because I watched him stagger back, his form blurry but still recognizable as he made for the window. Clambering over it, he spat over his shoulder. "I'll be back, and then you'll be *mine*."

Then he dropped out, scrambling away just in time for Thomas to wheel inside the room, Naomi at his feet with the hair all the way up her back raised in defense.

I pointed shakily to the window, still trying to blink back tears. "He went that way, I managed to clip him with a knife, but it wasn't enough and—"

I hardly pulled in air between words, my adrenaline-fueled babble only coming to a stop when a firm chest pressed against my mouth. Thomas's chest, specifically.

His arms wrapped tight around me, the safety I'd ached for coming to curl around me like a shield as I shuddered against him. The stress and fear oozed away, exhaustion taking its place as I slumped bonelessly against him.

He didn't run after Steven like I expected. Instead, he tightened his grip and brushed a kiss to my head. "Deep breaths, Virginia. You're all right; you did great. I'll call the cops and get them here. Maybe Richard will even show up to handle this. Just keep breathing."

I hadn't realized until then how *not* steady my breathing was, my lungs burning from the short gasps of air as Thomas's hand stroked up and down my back. When I struggled to take in air at a slower rate, he spoke while one of his hands wrestled his phone out.

"Match mine if you're having trouble."

I did, ear pressed flat to his chest as I forced my raspy inhales into time with his. The thunderous beat of his heart under my ear soothed some of the frantic urge to run, my shoulders easing from their tight line as I all but melted against him.

Everything was okay now, Thomas was here, and nothing would hurt me.

Tangling my arms around him in a crushing hug, I let the tears fall, feeling relief that it was over–at least for now–making my head spin.

He didn't miss a beat, gently leading me to the couch in the living room before sitting so I could comfortably curl against him. Once I was tucked into his chest, something soft brushed my leg, nearly sending me out of my skin.

Bello watched me with concern, his body purring like an engine as he wiggled his way against my side to offer comfort. I trailed fingers through his fur, only pausing when Naomi hopped up onto the couch next to us, her tongue sliding against my cheek in greeting.

Thomas didn't comment on suddenly having quite a bit more weight on him, instead choosing to shift to be more comfortable as he explained everything to whom I assumed was the dispatch officer. Sinking into his chest, I reveled in the bubble of safety now encasing us.

Things were far from over, but at least now I could breathe. Had to be happy with the little things.

Chapter 16

Richard hovered a few feet away, face set in a scowl as he finished writing down everything that's happened.

"I'll station a car outside your house tonight and get working on catching this guy. He's already getting sloppy and the blood on the cleaver should give us plenty of DNA evidence. Once we get a hold of him again, he's toast," he said, the words soothing almost as much as Thomas's gentle stroking moving up and down my back.

Forcing a shaky breath out of my lungs, I nodded. "Thank God. I'm beyond ready to never deal with this mess again. Will he get life this time or just another couple of years?"

After the mess he'd caused, I'd like to think they'd *keep* him in there, but I knew stalking wasn't treated as seriously as other crimes. Sure enough, Richard grimaced.

"It will depend. He's already bothered you again after his first time being put away, which means it'll bring his previous third-degree felony up to a second-degree one. The maximum sentence for those are twenty years in prison with fines of up to ten thousand dollars. But it depends on the lawyer, our evidence, and the judge."

Great, so it all revolved around a judge. The last one I'd had was sympathetic, but who's to say this one would be?

Apparently, Richard caught the unease in my face because he waved. "You don't have to worry on that front, I know the judge here, and he's a good man. Besides, he has daughters, nieces, and even a granddaughter now. I sincerely doubt he'll be taking this lightly."

Relief swept through me at that.

Nothing inspired empathy like having a family who could go through similar circumstances.

Giving a weak nod to Richard, I sank back into Thomas's side, fighting the urge to roll into him and hide from the world. I couldn't do that, no matter how nice it sounded.

I couldn't let Steven win like that.

Bello laid down with Naomi in the corner of the couch, the pair content to give us space as Richard finished the last of the wrap-up he needed to do. Once done, he leveled a sympathetic smile my way. "I'm going to leave and get all the paperwork started. Try to lay low, all right?"

I hummed, not having the energy for more than that. Richard didn't seem to mind, his attention shifting to Thomas, who rested at my back.

"If possible, I'd advise you to stay nearby. I know you've been working with Helena a lot trying to get the rescue up and rolling, but everything about this is making my skin crawl."

I completely agree, though in my case, it was fair to say I was *highly* biased.

Thomas grunted, shooting a look my way before shaking his head. "I'll do that, not like I mind spending time with my girl, and Helena will understand. Thanks for coming, Dick." His tone twinged with the familiar teasing only siblings could pull off, and his brother rolled his eyes.

"Yeah, yeah. I'm getting out of here. I have plenty of paperwork to do now."

I finally snapped back to the present, clearing my throat. "Sorry, I can only imagine."

Richard shook his head, patting my shoulder with an affectionate smile. "Don't worry about it. Better than going back to an empty apartment, and if it helps keep you safe, then it's more than worth it."

I nodded, watching his back as he left. Out the window, I saw him talk to another man in uniform, the stranger nodding before settling down in the car.

That was going to spike my paranoia through the roof, but I wouldn't turn my nose up at having someone nearby and ready in case things went south.

I didn't have to like it to know it was necessary.

Leaning back into Thomas, I slid down a bit and sighed. "What are the odds we can hide for the next month?"

His arm wound around my waist, offering the only stable thing in my life right now, as he brushed a kiss to my head. "Unlikely, given your work, but I'll be more than happy to hole up with you whenever you're not working."

Well, at least there was that. Can't look a gift horse in the mouth.

Sneaking a long glance back at the bathroom, I looked up at him and asked. "I'm going to take a bath, do you need anything before I do?"

Usually, I'd just ask him to join me, but right now, I needed half an hour of solitude to get my head on straight. He must have seen that because he shook his head.

"Nope, I think I'll make some baked goods for you, though. It doesn't make *everything* better, but it feels nicer to cry with cookies than without."

My lips twitched up in a valiant effort before dropping again. I shouldn't be surprised; he was absolutely the sort to bake me something to improve my mood.

Nodding, I tugged him down by his shirt to peck his cheek. "Thank you, once I get out, I'll be looking forward to that and maybe cuddling with a movie?" It ended with a question, but Thomas only smiled.

"Sounds like a fine way to end the day to me. You get your bath started and I'll handle the rest," he said, gently shooing me toward the bathroom.

I didn't bother fighting. The past few hours' worth of tension had me in so many knots that *everything* hurt, and the sooner I soaked that away, the better.

Bello hopped down from his place curled with Naomi, fluffy tail swishing with every step as he followed me to the bathroom as was our tradition whenever things were tense.

My little guard kitty.

I hadn't magically forgotten the part he'd played in saving me, and I was definitely going to be getting him some fresh fish for it.

Calling over my shoulder, I addressed that. "Thomas, remind me to pick up fish from the grocery store next time I go?"

Even through the walls, I heard his confusion. "I thought you hated fish?"

Warmth dusted through me that he'd remembered before I answered, fumbling with the knobs on the bathtub absentmindedly, "I do, but Bello more than earned it with how he attacked Steven."

A beat of silence came before he grunted his agreement, something that may have been "good kitty" distantly sounding through the walls. I didn't bother asking him to repeat it. If he wanted me to hear it, he would have spoken louder.

Instead, I turned my focus to the bath and my furred guardian. Well, one of two now, I guess. Naomi wouldn't want to be left out.

Chapter 17

Dragging a towel through my hair to dry it, I moved to the living room feeling ten times better already. The soreness from Thomas and my earlier activities was overshadowed now with a part less pleasant tenderness that only came from muscle tension and stress, but there was nothing I could do about that.

Though I might be able to beg a massage off Thomas if I asked nicely.

Shelving that thought to consider more later, I walked into the living room, only to freeze at the many bodies now crowding it.

Almost every last one of the Holliman family was here. Philip was absent, as was Richard–for obvious, paperwork-related reasons– and Simon wasn't here but other than that? The whole clan was seated on various couches or hovering behind them.

Finn sat to the side, a tray of what looked like some kind of cheese and beef wrap on his lap, with Thomas on the same couch with a massive platter of cookies on his.

The other couch housed Vincent, Adam, and to my surprise, their father. Penelope hovered behind them, but the second I came in, she was at my side, frown pulled down into a worried scowl.

"I'm sorry for dropping in like this, dear, but gossip spreads like wildfire in this town and hearing that-that *thug* was here and bothering you…I had to come and check on you. When Juan saw me leaving, he wanted to come, and then the boys got wind of it and wanted to check on you as well."

Her hands rang in her shirt, a nervous tick I had too, and without a second of thought, I flung my arms around her in a hug.

While I hadn't planned on interacting with so many people right now, the concern I could see on every last one of their faces touched me.

Family, they were here to support me, and as I sank into Penelope's arms, some of the sick tension faded back.

I have a family now.

Again hot tears burned the back of my eyes, but before I could blink them back, Penelope stroked a hand down my back and soothed. "It's all right; cry it out, honey. Better not to keep it inside. None of my boys would ever judge you for it, and if they *did*…Well, I'd be sure to put their behinds right back in line."

A watery laugh wrangled from my lungs as I let the flood go, hiding my face in her shoulder as her natural motherly air soothed an old burn I hadn't even realized still stung.

After a minute, I peaked my eyes open and took in the others in the room. Just like she said, not one of them was judging, though Finn did take the moment to crack a joke, throwing a playful wink my way when he noticed me watching.

"Bet your sweet behind we would never do that. No doubt, Ma will have us over her knee just like olden days. Doesn't matter how much time passes, not to mention your loverboy there would *geld* us." I snorted to that, Thomas's form rising to come closer as his mother pulled away.

His arm slid around my waist in the familiar sign of comfort before Finn tacked on, his impish smile fading into a softer, affectionate one.

"And while I can't speak for everyone else here, I'd geld *myself* if I said something to hurt you. You're too nice for it, even without being attached to my dear brother there."

That got nods all around, the solidarity between them making my lips twitch up as I brushed the last of the tears dried, and I leaned into Thomas.

"Thank you; I wouldn't want to hurt any of you either..." My eyes trailed down to the platters now sitting on the table and changed the subject. "So, what are those?"

Finn's smile stretched into a wide grin, moving to offer both of them to me with a flourish. "Food for the lady. Nothing makes a bad situation better like food. When I heard what was happening, I made the beef rolls. Apparently, the lover boy had the same idea."

Snagging one, I popped it into my mouth and hummed at the explosion of flavor. "It's delicious. If you don't have it on your menu you might want to reconsider."

Finn tilted his head, eyes flicking down to the rolls curiously before shrugging. "I hadn't considered it but I'll have to now that my potential future sister-in-law loves it so much."

He gave another wink before Penelope stepped in to gently herd him toward the couch again. "All right, that's enough out of you. Sit down and behave yourself."

Finn did without a second of hesitation, his mother chuckling fondly with a shake of her head. "Just like your papá, always joking around." She lightly shook her head, amusement clear as she patted Juan's hand.

The man only smiled adoringly down at her, shrugging at the accurate statement. "What can I say? I can't handle seeing a woman sad, nothing wrong with that."

She tugged him into a kiss, the open love between them wrapping a blanket around my heart. Sneaking a glance up at Thomas, I froze when I caught his eyes.

Would we be like that someday?

I definitely didn't mind the thought, and if the mild twitch of his lips was any indication, he didn't either. Bending low enough for his mouth to brush my ear, he muttered. "They're goals for the future, aren't they?"

I nodded, melting into him before his next words broke the warm gooey feelings, something hotter sliding in their place as he lowered his tone and continued. "My Spanish is rusty, but let me see if

I remember this at least..." Tightening his arm around my waist, he rumbled. "I adore you, mi corazón."

The foreign word rolled off his tongue, stroking down my spine as a gush of warmth settled in my chest. Oh, I was going to get in *so* much trouble over that.

Thomas grinned as if he could hear my thoughts but mercifully didn't comment. Instead, he turned his attention back to his parents and the cloud of happiness around them.

After a second, I did too. They really were goals, and maybe, in a few years, they could be parent goals too. I wasn't ready for kids, not with everything going on and how new our relationship was, but watching them now, I could imagine how doting they'd been.

A tight ache twisted in my chest at the thought, but before it could get out of hand, I yanked it back.

I didn't even know Thomas's thoughts on kids yet, and I couldn't start making goo-goo eyes. Another pulse of that tightness came, and I gave in.

Soon, I'd bring up the topic just so I knew what kind of future we were looking at. Thomas wasn't the sort to run screaming at the mention of something he wasn't interested in and I'd be sure he knew I wasn't pressuring him.

For now, though, I just want to soak in the pleasantness of the present.

Chapter 18

I sat bolt upright, the nightmare still clinging to the edges of my mind.

Once my breathing evened out, I groaned, flopping back to the bed in frustration.

Shelving the frustration, I reached out for Thomas, only to freeze at the empty bed next to me. That was odd; he'd been the sort to knock out like a rock before I fell asleep. Nothing short of touch would wake him.

Maybe he'd had to use the restroom?

Even as I thought it, a sound from the kitchen came and I inched toward the edge of the bed. Or maybe he'd wanted a snack. Either way, it wasn't difficult to follow him.

Giving Naomi and Bello pats as I passed, the duo curled contently at the foot of the bed, I breezed into the kitchen. As I thought, Thomas sat on one of the stools with a mug of something clasped in his hand. What I didn't expect was the exhaustion hanging off him like a shroud.

Worry cleared away the last bits of my sleep and I sank into the seat next to him, his smile tired but genuine when he leveled it on me.

"All good, mi corazón?" he asked.

It tugged at my heart how he worried even while looking like he'd been hit by a train. Scooting closer, I kissed his head and shrugged.

"Nightmare. What about you?" I asked, watching his face twist into a grimace. At first I thought he'd brush it off, but after a long minute, he sighed.

"The same. Been having them off and on since coming back to the states, but this is the first one in a while."

Without thinking, my head dropped to his shoulder and I nodded. "Makes sense. Those kinds of things don't just go away. Have you been feeling cagey lately in crowds?"

His hefty sigh was just as much an answer as his words. "Yeah, more so than usual too. I thought it would just go back to how it used to be before I left, but it's only getting worse." The tone was almost lost, and I instinctively answered.

"You know, therapy might benefit you. No pressure or anything, just saying," I offered, watching as Thomas dragged a tired hand through his hair.

He didn't tense or snarl as others had in the past when confronted with therapy. Instead, he leveled a tired look my way. "I may have to. I want to be able to take you places without feeling like a bomb about to go off."

I patted his arm, cuddling closer as I continued. "If it'll make you feel better, I could go in too? I'm the only therapist here in town so we'd have to go to the next one over. I was told to go after the first time Steven struck, but I ignored it. Maybe it's time we both went."

I'd considered going before, the seemingly unending paranoia getting old after no time at all, but like with the defense classes, something always seemed to come up at a bad time.

But maybe this was a sign it was time for both of us.

Thomas stayed quiet for a long minute before he squeezed my hand. "Sounds like a plan. When do you have off next and we can schedule with a therapist?"

I mentally slid over my schedule before answering. "Tuesday, does that work?"

He didn't hesitate. "Yup. Now come on, we can talk more about this later. We're both gonna need sleep for tomorrow." Thomas paused, seeming to consider something before turning to face me. "I meant to ask earlier, but do you mind me staying over every night? Like overnight. I wanted to ask before, but with everything, I'd forgotten."

He didn't add the last bit out loud, but we were both thinking it.

And with Steven out, I don't want you to be alone.

While I would have accepted without that hanging over our heads, now that things were changing and becoming more dangerous, I had another reason not to mind having him here.

Nodding, I leaned into him as the hard line of his shoulders eased. "Sounds fine by me. I mean, having you wrapped around me at night more often?" I paused to give a fake shudder, "How ever will I survive?"

His lips twitched up to that before he led us back to my room. "Dunno, it's gonna be tough but we'll make it through."

It was only when we were both curled in bed, his body heat seeping through to tug the last of the tension away, that I remembered my earlier thoughts about kids. Was now a good time to bring it up, though? Things have been insane lately.

But would I keep chickening out if I didn't just make myself do it?

After a bit of thought, I knew the answer. I would. So with that in mind, I nudged into Thomas and asked. "You still awake?"

One of his eyes flicked open, sharp with alertness and not an ounce of drowsiness showing. "Yeah?"

Biting my lip, I chose my words carefully. "I have a question, but I'm not sure how to ask it. It's pretty personal and I don't want to make you feel pressured."

One of his brows ticked up to that. "Doubt you ever could, but ask. If I don't want to answer, I'll say so," he said, eyes intent on me as he shifted to give me his full attention.

Well, now or never. Sucking in a breath and holding it, I continued. "What are your thoughts on kids? Eventually." I added the last bit hastily, not wanting him to think I meant *now*. I wasn't ready for them now, but maybe sometime in the future.

Understanding flashed behind his eyes before a quiet contemplation took over. Silence ticked by, and after a few moments, my nerves stretched to the breaking point. Just as I went to take it back, though, he answered, his hand coming down to clasp mine.

"Honestly? I hadn't thought about it. I've been in the military so long that I wrote off having a family."

Huh?

My brow furrowed as I tried to figure out what he meant. "Your Dad had you guys while he was in the military, didn't he?" I asked, hoping for clarification.

The last thing I expected was for Thomas's face to shut down. All emotion leaked out until a grimace remained, the sudden coldness sending unease straight down my spine.

I knew why when he spoke again.

His hand trailed down my back, stroking in rhythm as he looked anywhere but me. "Don't tell Dad I said this, all right?" I nodded, and he continued. "I love my parents, but growing up without Dad, having to watch Mom juggle it all because he was away?"

He shook his head. "I could never do that to someone. From the time I was a teen to now, I know that. I couldn't make a woman—especially *my* woman—be a single parent. And I couldn't do it to my kids either. I know from the other end of that deal how bad it is."

As he spoke, his eyes became far away, trapped in memories from who knows how long ago. "I remember every missed birthday, Christmas, and Thanksgiving. I remember the empty chair when Vincent graduated. Hell, the empty chair when *most* of us graduated. The only reason he came back and was there for mine, Adam's, and

Richard's was because he was forcibly discharged with an injury. He wouldn't have made it otherwise."

His mouth twisted at the painful memories. "Richard was fourteen when that happened, still young enough to actually *have* our father in his life. Adam and I were sixteen, and it was harder to just accept that he was back. To a point, we always expected him to leave again."

I hadn't even considered that, but maybe I should have. Yes, Juan had served many years in the military and that was an honorable thing, but he'd also left behind *so many* minutes with his family to have that.

Thinking back on how touchy he was with his sons–always making sure to give them a hug before they had to leave–something clicked into place. He was still trying to make up for lost time.

The thought squeezed my heart and without hesitation, I curled closer to Thomas, a hand rising to stroke his cheek. "I see where you're coming from now. I wouldn't want to make anyone live like that either, but now that you're out?"

I gently nudged the conversation into a less painful direction. He'd needed to say this, that much I knew, but it was out now, and every second the pain lingered on his face was one too many for me.

Some of the weight left his face as he smiled, adoration bubbling to the surface as his eyes focused back on me.

"Now that I'm out, I could see it. I always wanted a family and, whenever you're ready, I am too," he said, dipping to trail a kiss from the tip of my ear down the line of my jaw. He paused at my cheek, beard scratching lightly as he hummed.

"Which leaves your opinion on it," he said, not a question but still kind of one.

Inching to curl into his arm, I answered. "I want one too, not *right now*, but maybe sometime within the next few years. I could see raising a family with you, and the more I think about it, the more *right* it feels."

His smile didn't slip as he nodded. "Same here, and I'm glad we talked about this."

So we were both hesitating, not surprising. Claiming my spot under his chin, the thump of his heartbeat soothing under my ear, I hummed. "It's out now. We can figure out the details when we hit that point. For now, I'm exhausted."

The nightmare had taken its toll, and every second, my lids dropped just that much more. Thomas chuckled, catching that, as he tightened his arms around me into a shield.

"Get some rest; I'll probably be following soon."

I grumbled something that may have been a good night before everything faded into the bliss of sleep.

Chapter 19

Weeks passed in what felt like blinks of an eye, Steven's threat hanging overhead as Richard hustled to get a case against him ready for when he was inevitably caught.

He'd said it was looking good, which was relieving. Apparently, he'd even mentioned this mess to the judge ahead of time and the judge seemed to be on our side.

Which just left catching Steven.

Everyone in town knew to keep an eye out for him now, but since that night in my house, he hadn't struck again.

Though that could be because Thomas was here more often than not.

While I didn't like the situation that'd caused it, I definitely wasn't complaining about having him around more. I'd never known how nice it was to have a *human* to cuddle with through the night.

Bello was always welcome in the pile, of course, and so was Naomi, but having Thomas's arms wrapped around me made everything feel all right.

As if hearing my thoughts, said arms hooked around my waist, pulling me back to the present and the mild buzz of noise around us.

Thomas smiled down at me, exhaustion hovering just below the surface. Not that I could blame him. We'd both gone to therapy today and it'd been harrowing for more than just me. After *that*, he'd mentioned a barn dance in town, both of us needing something light-hearted after the start to the day.

He was right. The music was upbeat and jaunty, not too many people crowding the place, and he'd even pulled me onto the floor once or twice for a dance. Of course, seeing him in jeans and boots had *nothing* to do with my enjoyment...

Well, it wasn't all of it at least.

Leaning back against him, I soaked in the peace of the moment. "Hey, how you holding up?" I asked. It was important to keep an eye on how he was doing. He'd made impressive strides over the past few weeks with crowds, but that didn't mean we should do too much at once.

Apparently, he agreed because after a long glance around at the music and people, he offered. "Decent, but we should probably head out soon." I caught the edge to his eyes and nodded. We were also getting better about communicating when one of us needed a break.

Stealing another glance around the room, I offered a hand. "One more dance and then we go home?"

Without hesitation, he nodded. "Perfect."

His hand curled around mine, the sheer size difference sending a shiver of awareness down my arm before he pulled me to the floor for one last dance.

I'd never pegged Thomas for the type to enjoy it, but as he swung me around with laughable ease, the dizzying spins dragging bubbling laughter up from my lungs, I knew we'd have to do this again sometime.

Even if it was just putting some music on our phones and dancing at home, I wanted to see that joy in his eyes more often.

The song started winding down, his arm settling around my waist as he pulled me into a dip just at the end. Biting back a laugh at my sudden almost upside-down position, I kissed his nose. "I'm *so* telling your brothers about this."

He shrugged, righting us again as he hooked our arms together and made for the door.

"Go for it. They already know I like dancing. Heck, almost all of them do. The only one who doesn't is Philip and that's because he can't do it. Anytime he tries, it comes across like a fish flopping around on land," he said, tone teasing as he poked fun at his brother.

I couldn't stop the snort at the mental image. "That's not nice. I'm sure he isn't *that* bad." I tried to come to Philip's rescue, only for Thomas to shake his head.

"He is, but the next time we have some big family shindig, you can see for yourself. Ma usually drags him into at least one dance, to his chagrin. If she doesn't, then Drew will."

I could imagine that.

Trailing my fingers to rest over his on the gear shift, I melted into the seat as we made our way home. We'd both made admirable progress over the past few weeks, and I wasn't afraid to say I was proud of us.

Thomas was handling crowds better and I was having fewer nightmares. We still had plenty of room to grow, but I'd be happy with every step we had in between.

In no time at all, the house pulled into sight and he stopped, sliding out to get my door as always. "How much do you want to bet Naomi is sulking over being left behind?" he asked, my arm automatically finding his as we made for the door.

I snorted. "Not a cent because that's exactly what she's doing. She's a daddy's girl to the bone and you can't convince me otherwise."

I'd seen that dog full-on *pout* when Thomas left; there was no doubt on the subject.

He didn't argue, giving me space to get the door as he shrugged. "I can't argue that."

The door clicked shut behind us and I braced for the furry bodies to come hurtling our way.

Only, they didn't come.

Sharing a confused glance with Thomas, I called, "Naomi, Bello, we're back!" I'd never needed to tell them that before; they always came running to greet us the second they heard the tires on the driveway.

Again, nothing.

Worry chewed on the back of my spine, inching higher with every passing minute. Before I could move further into the house, Thomas gently pulled me back.

The smile from before was gone, his face set in a mask of grimness as he nudged me toward the door. "Stay here; I'm going to check it out. I don't like how the air feels and I'm not risking you."

If it weren't for the fact Steven was still very much a problem, I would argue with him, but I wasn't stupid. Thomas was trained by the military, and I had *no* training. If Steven was here, then he was banking on me running in.

I wouldn't give him the satisfaction.

I nodded, leaning against the wall as Thomas pulled the gun he always carried and started to check the rest of the house.

It was hardly a minute later when I heard it, laughter.

Specifically, Thomas's deep rolling one.

Confusion washed away the fear from before as I called back, "Is everything all right?"

I didn't have to wait long before Thomas responded, humor still shaking his voice. "Yeah, it's all great. Come look for yourself. Trust me, the furry brats *definitely* have the situation handled."

What was he talking about?

Breezing into the room, I froze at the scene in front of me

Steven laid on the ground, his arms above his head and every muscle frozen. His hair was a mess, thrown in every direction, and blood splashed across his front like an old horror film.

But that wasn't why Thomas had laughed. No, he'd laughed because Bello sat perched on his face, claws dug into the base as he leisurely cleaned himself on Steven's head.

And if that wasn't a hilarious picture on its own, Naomi had taken it upon herself to detain Steven until we got back. Namely, she'd sunk teeth directly into his groin. At least that explained why Steven had gone still so willingly.

One didn't play around when their genitals were in danger, after all.

Biting back my own snort at the scene, I reached for my phone with a shake of my head. "Talk about karma."

Thomas nodded, though he pouted when he noticed my phone. "Do we *have* to call Richard right away? I'm enjoying this, and I think Naomi is too, aren't you, girl?"

In response, the dog's tail wagged, but she didn't loosen her grip. Steven finally spoke at that, his voice cracking high with fear.

"Call the pigs! Call them before the fucking mutt eats my junk," he shouted, eyes comically wide as Naomi growled.

I patted Thomas's arm as I dialed. "As much as I'm enjoying this—and I am, make no mistake—I don't want *that* in Naomi's mouth for any longer than absolutely necessary. Who knows where it's been?"

Thomas visibly considered that before heaving a long, put upon sigh. "Fine, you have a point. Doesn't mean I can't enjoy every minute of this until my brother shows up. Can we at least ask him to drive slowly?"

I shrugged, keeping one eye on Steven as I answered. "We'll see if he's even working today."

It took hardly five minutes before Richard was on his way, completely ignoring Thomas's wish for him to drive slower. I couldn't blame him though. After everything Steven had caused, I just wanted him put away.

No matter how satisfying this sight was, I wanted everything to be over more.

Thankfully, Richard made it in record time, the car pulling up as he and his partner jumped out. I got the door for them, waving back to where Steven was pinned down as I addressed Richard. "He's in there, though you'll need to get Thomas to call off Naomi."

One of his brows rose to that, but he didn't comment. Instead, he led the way in, only pausing when he saw the position Steven had landed himself in.

His partner snorted, a smile twitching across his lips as he got handcuffs out. "I'm tempted to let him stay like that, to be honest."

Before Thomas could say anything, Steven sneered, trying to spit at Richard and his partner's shoes.

"I shouldn't be surprised. You pigs enjoy causing pain whenever possible."

He *had* to be joking.

Storming past the others, I towered over Steven and hissed. "That is absolutely *rich* coming from you! You stalked me relentlessly, violated my home, tried to do *worse,* and now you have the balls to say that to them?"

Not giving him a chance to respond, I looked to Thomas and hissed, "Call Naomi off."

Apparently, he either figured out what I was going to do or he knew I was lethally pissed because he did without hesitation. Once she was safely out of harm's way, I reeled my leg back and slammed it full force between Steven's thighs.

His howl split the air, Richard's choked laugh overshadowed by it as he and his partner gently moved to get between my stalker and me.

His partner cuffed Steven, eyes sparkling with amusement as he looked at Thomas. "Got one hell of a spitfire there. Watch your gonads, my man."

Before I could snarl that he had no reason to be afraid for them, Thomas's arm wound around my waist and he shook his head. "Bud, if I ever do something to warrant that ball-shot, I won't be running from it. Besides, even if I escaped Virginia, Ma would do considerably worse when *she* got a hold on me."

From what I knew of Penelope, he wasn't lying.

Apparently, Richard's partner knew that too because he nodded. "Fair, now then. I'm going to bring this slime back to the station. You got the rest, Dick?"

Richard rolled his eyes, Apparently, giving up on getting rid of that nickname, as he nodded. "Yeah, I do. Now get out of here with him. I'll get their statements in the meantime. It'll be a nice change from all the paperwork I've been doing lately."

The other man nodded, gently stroking Bello's head when my kitty finally left his perch on Steven's face, before leaving. Once they were gone, I slumped back against Thomas, the man automatically moving to catch me.

Adrenaline swarmed, buzzing loudly in my ears as I focused on breathing. What would have happened if Thomas hadn't left Naomi here?

Would he have hurt Bello? Waited here for me and struck?

A shudder slid up my spine at the thought. Considering what he'd tried to do last time, I knew what his goal would be now, and I could only be grateful for how things turned out.

Richard leveled an understanding smile my way as he pulled out his trusty pad of paper. "I know the last thing you want is to think about what happened, but afterward, we can finally get to putting this creep away. So, I need you both to tell me in as much detail as you can, what happened here."

I did, everything fading back into a weird surreally as I heard Thomas do the same. I was distantly aware of Richard saying something and leaving, but it was only when Thomas sat me down on my bed that I snapped back to the present.

Concern knit his brow. Bello and Naomi pressed on either side of him as his fingers stroked my palms. When he noticed I was back in the present, he sighed.

"There you are, was starting to think I'd need to call Philip," he said, relief clear in every syllable as I slumped bonelessly against his side.

No, that wasn't necessary, though I appreciated the thought. Gripping his hand, I shook the last of the haze away and smiled.

"I'm all right, just…stunned. I guess. I knew he would strike again; I just didn't expect it to happen like this."

With Naomi's teeth buried into his groin.

Thomas chuckled, Apparently, thinking much the same as he eased both of us back to lie on the bed. "Neither did I, but I think it's poetic justice for all the hell he put you through. No one should have to have gone through that, least of all you."

The hard edge of protectiveness peaked out in his tone before I wiggled up to kiss his brow. "Don't over think it. It's done now, he's going to be out of our lives, and I get to focus on you. That's all that matters," I said, stroking his cheek as the tension slowly bled off.

An arm wound around my back, tugging me closer as he nodded. "True. Maybe after it's all settled, I can bring you out dancing again, or even a concert. I think one of those is coming up soon, though it's a bit of a drive to get there."

A concert sounded fun, but…

"Are you sure you'd be all right with that? Lots of people, no elbow room, and the music is *loud*." I asked, wanting to make sure he knew what he was getting into.

He nodded without a speck of hesitation. "I'm sure, and if things start to be too much, then we can leave. I think I'll be all right, though."

I relaxed, trusting him to his word as I sank into his chest and soaked in the bliss of the moment. Things weren't over yet, we still had to deal with court and all that, but just the knowledge that Steven wasn't on the streets anymore was enough to soothe me.

No more late-night paranoia, always checking the windows for what might be a silhouette. No more worrying about when *he* would strike.

Just Thomas and I, figuring out our lives together.

I could definitely get behind that.

Epilogue

The market was buzzing with activity as Thomas and I made our way down each aisle. He'd insisted on coming in today despite how busy it was and so far he seemed to be handling it well.

Our arms stayed locked together, his other hand guiding the cart as we moved. He was tense but not ready to bolt. His eyes swept the area around us before glancing down at me. "What else do we need?" he asked, voice strained but not asking to leave yet.

If he didn't soon, I'd send him out regardless. There was a difference between pushing your boundaries and punishing yourself.

Still, I'd give him a bit longer.

Doing another look over the list, I answered. "We're about halfway through. There's still laundry detergent, dog food, cat food, and then ice cream."

The ice cream could be ignored if it came down to it, but the others were non-negotiable.

Thomas nodded, angling the cart toward the pet aisle. "I can see you worrying from here and I'm all right. A bit edgier than I'd prefer, but still not freaking out. I can handle the pet aisle and the laundry detergent," he said, voice petering off as he added. "I might need to wait outside by the time we get to the ice cream, though."

I squeezed his arm, pride welling in my chest that he'd admit that. "That's fine, it's not important and we can come back on a different day for it. Let's just focus on getting the pet food and—"

"You stupid bitch, if you hadn't gotten the wrong thing the first time, then we wouldn't have had to come now!"

The shout cut me off, instinct spinning me around to face the voice as Thomas tensed, arm hesitating closer to his belt where his gun usually was. I gripped his arm, keeping it in mine as we took in the person who'd shouted.

A man stood not far, eyes ablaze with rage as he glared at a woman.

A very familiar woman.

Icy understanding hit as Scarlet's form came into clarity, her back to us as she raised her hands in appeasement. I could just barely hear her response.

"I know, and I offered to come alone, but you insisted. Lower your voice before someone hears—" She'd raised her hands as if to plead with him, but before she could finish her sentence, a sharp *CRACK* sounded through the air, his fist meeting her cheek and sending her staggering back.

I straightened, letting Thomas go as the air crackled with tension and he braced, ready to step in at a moment's notice.

Fingering my phone, I got ready to pull it out, only for the man to catch our eyes and freeze. When his gaze lingered up to Thomas's, pure hate blazed to life.

Shoving past Scarlet, the woman sent careening into the shelf with an echoing crash, he made for us. Thomas yanked me behind him, arms tensing as the man stopped right in front of him.

Now that he was closer, I noticed the striking resemblance to Scarlet as a sinking understanding hit. This was her father. Their face shape and characteristics were too similar to be anything else, though his hair was dusted in gray.

And he'd hit her.

Suddenly, our suspicions came racing back, souring my stomach. We were at least partially right; she was being abused. There was no telling if that was linked to her initial breaking things off with Richard, but a niggling feeling at the back of my mind said it was.

I didn't have a chance to consider it more before the man leaned in, the scent of booze coming off him in waves as he hissed.

"Bold of you to show your fucking face to me, Holliman."

Shit, he was going to pick a fight. Stealing a glance up at Thomas, I grimaced at the tense line of his shoulders. Not good.

He'd already been having trouble before this. The addition of this idiot was going to push him over.

Latching onto his arm, I tried to tug him back as I desperately motioned for security to get *over here*. They started our way, but not before Thomas snarled.

"I'm allowed to go anywhere in this town, old man. And considering what I just saw, I wouldn't sound so righteous. The judge doesn't take well to women *or* child beaters, and you just did both."

His tone was three degrees above freezing and it put me on edge. We needed to get out of here before someone threw a punch.

Unfortunately, the man scoffed. "You didn't see jack shit, and she won't say anything. I ensured it." At that, he turned to face Scarlet, who was just getting her feet back under her from the hit.

"Ain't that right, girl? Nothing happened here." His tone oozed with threat, and I fought the urge to get between them like she'd done for me with that creep Jake.

To my disbelief, her eyes stayed locked on the ground, and she nodded. "Right, we were just…having a disagreement. We should get our things and head home."

Before I could say anything, one of the security guards came forward, eyeing Scarlet and her father with a sneer. "Any trouble here, gentlemen?"

Scarlet's father eyed Thomas for a long minute before shaking his head. "No, nothing at all. We were just shopping."

The security guard eyed him with clear disbelief but let it drop. "Good, wouldn't want to get the deputy involved."

Wrong thing to say.

Scarlet's father's eyes blazed again, his daughter stiffening behind him as he spat. "No need to get *him* here. One Holliman is more than enough per day for me. Scarlet, let's get out of here."

He didn't give her a chance to follow, his grip latching onto her arm and forcibly dragging her out. I grit my teeth, forcing myself not to say anything as Thomas waved off the security guard. Once we were alone again, I shuddered.

"Looks like we were right," I said, hating every word of it.

Thomas nodded, grimacing firmly in place as he spoke. "Yeah. I'll mention that to Richard later, but for now, there's nothing we can do. Technically, there's nothing we can do even afterward. Richard can try to talk to Scarlet, but if she doesn't tell him anything…"

I nodded. Then it wouldn't do any good. She had to speak up or nothing would stick against her father. And considering how she'd reacted just now? That wasn't going to happen.

Hooking my arm with his again, I moved us over to grab the dog and cat food, noting the slight tremor rolling through his frame with a sigh. The laundry detergent would have to wait too. If it came down to it I could probably ask one of his brothers to borrow theirs if we didn't have a chance to get out again soon, but hopefully, it wouldn't come to that.

Thankfully, the rest of the shopping trip went well, Thomas didn't ask why I skipped the laundry aisle, and I took that as his agreement that we needed to go *now*. It was only after we made it to the parking lot that things went pear-shaped…as they do.

Just as we put the last bag into the truck, an ear-splitting screech cut through the air. One second I was behind the truck next to our cart. The next, Thomas had grabbed me and thrown both of us to the ground.

From underneath him, I could hear dozens of people running, shouts slowly trickling through the buzzing in my ears as I looked up at Thomas. His eyes were far away, frame tense as looked around us for enemies that weren't there.

Shit. Today had been too much for him.

Gently tracing his cheek, I soothed, hoping it would pull him back. "Thomas, look at me, honey."

At first it was as if he didn't hear, but after a long minute, his eyes drifted to mine. Stroking his beard, I continued. "We're all right, just breathe for me."

He did, his chest heaving with a massive breath as he blinked, the dark edge to his eyes fading back as he did another sweep around us. This time he was in the present and when he finally sat up, gently helping me as well, I sighed in relief.

Okay, that was it. After we got home, I was locking the door and calling it a day.

Just as we were both standing again, I noticed the crowd of people not far off. It was only when one of them moved to the side that I realized what'd happened.

There'd been a car crash. What looked to be a drunk driver had plowed into one of the parked cars. The distant wail of ambulance sirens hit, but when I noticed who stood next to the car, none of that mattered.

Scarlet leaned against the mangled truck, her face paper white while clutching her chest. Her eyes were riveted on the driver's seat of the car she leaned against, and it was only then that I realized something. Her father wasn't with her.

Slowly looking where she was, I could just see the flash of familiar graying hair before the ambulance skidded to a stop nearby and started their work.

I caught snippets of the conversation when they loaded her father into the ambulance. "Head injury." "Low heart rate." "Emergency operation."

Scarlet hadn't moved once since the entire thing happened, as if too frozen to even breathe. It was only when one of the EMTs gently pulled her into the same ambulance that I snapped back to the present.

Looking up at Thomas, his face just as pale as mine probably was, I choked out.

"We need to talk to Richard. Today."

He nodded, helping me into his truck before loping back to his seat. Things were moving faster now, but through it all, only one thought remained.

Scarlet's father was in the hospital after hitting his daughter. If he *had* been abusing her, then she was temporarily safe until he got out. If she wasn't telling Richard something thanks to a threat from her dad, then now was our chance.

I could only hope she'd take it.

END OF BOOK 1

Book 2 in The Holliman Brothers Series, **Richard's Menidng Desire** tells the story of High School Sweethearts Richard and Scarlet, that were Forced Apart due to some dangerous circumstances. Scarlet decided to kept this from Richard thinking she was protecting him but only left him completely heart broken and confused why they broke up. Coping with this loss, Richard became the town Playboy, which was completely out to character for him.

Living in the same Small Town was torcher for both of them, but after years apart, Scarlet thought the threat was finally gone and went to Richard to explain after all this time. Only to realize that she now had a new danger arise. Richard was hesitant to even hear Scarlet out, but it was his duty to keep her safe as a Sheriff Deputy from this new danger. Will their time apart and betray on both sides be too much for this couple? Or will their Close Proximity bring them back together?

Next book in the series:
Richad's Mending Desire
The Holliman Brothers Book 2

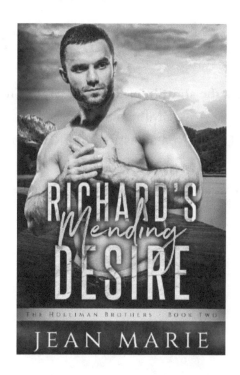

More Books From The Holliman Brothers Series

Did you miss the short book PREQUEL to The Holliman Brothers Series?

Read Adam's Undiscovered Passion for FREE! Only available in ebook.

Visit www.jeanmariebooks.com to get yours or email jm@jeanmariebooks.com

There are 6 books total in The Holliman Brothers Series. All standalone books but best if read in order for maximum enjoyment:

- Adam's Undiscovered Passion - Free short Prequel to The Holliman Brothers Series (only available in ebook - see previous page for info)

Books 1-5 of The Holliman Brothers are available on Amazon for purchase in Paperback or Ebook.

- Thomas' Rescued Heart - Book 1 The Holliman Brothers Series
- Richard's Mending Desire - Book 2 The Holliman Brothers Series
- Philip's Unfathomed Connection - Book 3 The Holliman Brothers Series
- Simon's Unchartered Intimacy - Book 4 The Holliman Brothers Series
- Finn's Hidden Destiny - Boon 5 The Holliman Brothers Series

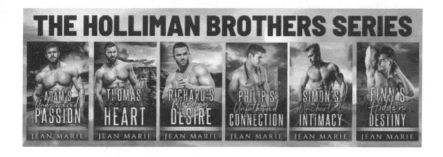

Other Series From Jean Marie

If you're loving The Holliman Brothers Series, you should also check out Lucky Luca Ranch Series. It's a similar Small Town Suspense Romance series but set on a Ranch. It's actually where the Holliman Family was first introduced in book 5 of Vincent's Bulletproof Secret. Vince Holliman and Clarice's story is one you're not going to want to miss, so grab your copies now! All books available on Amazon in Paperback or Ebook:

Gabriel's Long Haul - Book 1 Lucky Luca Ranch Series
Bruce's Troubled Temptation - Book 2 Lucky Luca Ranch Series
Edmund's Last Heartbreak - Book 3 Lucky Luca Ranch Series
Ron's Unexpected Salvation - Book 4 Lucky Luca Ranch Series
Vincent's Bulletproof Secret - Book 4 Lucky Luca Ranch Series

Jean Marie also writes MC Romances. But not your typical Motorcycle Club Romances, it's more of Sexy Alpha Men with big hearts. They'll do anything to protect their women, their club brothers and their community. It's about loyalty, respect, and honor. So if MC Romances aren't something you're particular into, just gives these a chance because I bet you'll enjoy!

Bone's Claim

FREE Short Story Prequel to the Red Spades MC Romance Series

Visit www.jeanmariebooks.com to get your copy or email jm@jeanmariebooks.com

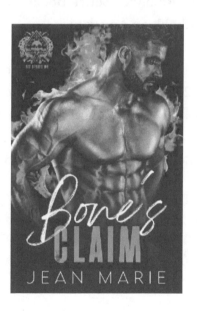

Red Spades MC Romance Series Books 1-3 are now available in Paperback and Ebook on Amazon:

Zerk's Mark - Book 1 Red Spades MC Romance Series
Beowulf's Fury - Book 2 Red Spades MC Romance Series
Einstein's Revenge - Book 3 Red Spades MC Romance Series

Wheel Mongers MC Romance Series Books 1-5 are now available in Paperback and Ebook on Amazon:

Axe's Havoc - Book 1 Wheel Mongers MC Romance Series
Joker's Oath - Book 2 Wheel Mongers MC Romance Series
Cowboy's Chaos- Book 3 Wheel Mongers MC Romance Series
Knuckles' Wreckage - Book 4 Wheel Mongers MC Romance Series
Uppercut's Ghost - Book 5 Wheel Mongers MC Romance Series

About Jean Marie

Jean Marie is an Action and Suspense Romance writer with an edge. Her books are realistic with a lot of emotion, and will take you on a roller coaster of a ride. Each book has is a full-length, standalone storyline and always has an HEA. They can always be read for FREE with Kindle Unlimited.

Follow Jean Marie on Facebook for updates, book teasers, and so much more!

facebook.com/jeanmariebooks/

Now on Tiktok!

tiktok.com/@jeanmariebooks

Have any feedback or book suggestions?

Email Jean Marie at jm@jeanmariebooks.com

Made in United States
Troutdale, OR
09/28/2024

23187721R00137